JACLYN AND THE BEANSTALK

Other Books by Mary Ting

International Sensory Assassin Network Series
ISAN
Soon to be a major motion picture

The Crossroads Saga
Crossroads
Between
Beyond
Eternity
Halo City

Descendant Prophecies Series
From Gods
From Deities
From Origins
From Titans

Secret Knights Series
The Angel Knights
The Chosen Knights
The Blessed Knights
The Sacred Knights

The Book of Watchers

JACLYN AND THE BEANSTALK

MARY TING

Jaclyn and the Beanstalk

This is a work of fiction. Names, characters, places, and incidents either are the product of the author's imagination or are used fictitiously.
Any resemblance to actual persons, living or dead, events or locales is entirely coincidental.

Original Cover Illustration by Sam Shearon

ISBN: 978-1-944109-74-5

VESUVIAN BOOKS

Published by Vesuvian Books
www.vesuvianbooks.com

Printed in the United States of America

10 9 8 7 6 5 4 3 2 1

Table of Contents

Chapter One
Sixteenth Century

Shrieks rent the peaceful night. I bolted upright and gulped air as if I had been under water too long. My heart raced as a white, ghost-like mist escaped my panting mouth. Despite the chill, sweat trickled down my forehead and dampened my back, causing the fabric of my chemise to stick.

I squinted through the darkness; moonlight faintly illuminated the storage chest and a nub of a candle was atop the plain table. In my room—*safe*. But my heart did not slow, for the cries still echoed in my mind.

Please, go away. Go away.

My head—a pounding mess.

Curling into a ball and covering my ears, I hummed a tune Mother used to sing. The song always had a way of comforting me, but it never made the noise go away.

Thinking the devil waited for me to lose my mind, to seize my soul, I whispered the Lord's Prayer. "...And forgive us our trespasses, as we forgive those who trespass against us. Lead us not into temptation, but deliver us from evil."

As the noises faded, I released my knees. Exhaustion consumed me and I found sleep once more.

"Rise, Jaclyn," Father hollered from the kitchen. "Time for your lesson."

No, no, no.

I squirmed lower under my coverlet and yawned.

Bodies shuffled and thumped in other rooms. Rubbing the sleep from my eyes, I shivered as frosty air pricked my bones. Outside my window, the sun glowed molten-gold through the cluster of gray clouds.

Perhaps the night before had been a dream. Can one dream the same dream for months on end?

I swept the night's occurrences to the back of my mind and pulled the bedclothes tighter. I shut my eyes against the light kissing my cheeks and thought only of rest until my chamber door creaked open.

The mattress shifted.

"Father." I flailed my arms and kicked uncontrollably, laughing and slapping his hands as he tickled my sides. "Cease, cease. I'm awake."

I sat up and clutched the coverlet, wishing to be honest with him about the nightmares. Swallowing the words, I gave him a sheepish smile. He had a belly full of worries and I did not wish to add mine. I would not have him think the devil damned my soul; Father's belief would make it true.

He'd aged right before my eyes. Even his garments—dark breeches and a forest-green tunic—drooped wearily, and his muddy black boots had cracked. Father's thick eyelashes touched his ruddy face when he looked down. His rough hands, callused and dirty from labor, cradled his favorite tatty, brown hat, and he poked his finger through a hole in the top.

"Are you well, Daughter?" The skin around his nut-brown eyes crinkled with concern, and his forehead creased.

No. I hear monsters at night. Something is wrong with your daughter.

"Yes." I disliked keeping the truth from him. "A little unwell, perhaps."

I smiled when the aroma of fresh baked bread wafted through the door, but cringed at the sight of rat droppings on the white linens—gifts from vermin in the thatch that had fallen from the roof.

Father raised his chin and wiggled his nose. "Generous this time, were they not?" He chuckled. "They left none for me last night."

I cursed under my breath, frowning. "They left me plenty."

"You're late abed this morning." Father rubbed his jaw, and pushed his fingers through the white streaks by his temple before placing the hat on his dark head. "Do you want to pass this morning?"

Closing my eyes, I wished my lassitude away. "Nay. I need to dress first." I plucked at my white chemise.

"Certainly. Clothe yourself and eat some of your mother's bread. I'll be tending to the horses." He ruffled my hair and shut the door behind him.

Determined to begin the day afresh and forget the previous night, I took out a boy's breeches and tunic from my chest. Mother had frowned when I wore them at first, but ceased when she grew tired of mending gowns.

Father had been training me to use a sword and other weapons, so I had no choice but to dress accordingly. Our only neighbors were hills and forest—no townspeople to scandalize.

Hunger pangs grew as I opened my chamber door. Just before I closed it behind me, I glanced about. I had smoothed the coverlet, shut the chest, and ensured nothing lay on the dirt floor. The small chamber left no room for a mess.

"You're awake at last."

Mother's smile and sky-blue eyes warmed me better than the fire under the big kettle.

I smiled back. "Good morning, Mother. Thank you for the delicious meal I'm about to eat."

A tankard of milk and a wooden trencher bearing a piece of bread with sweet butter had been set on the table. After I said grace, Mother tugged at my long, brown hair as I devoured my meal.

"You're sixteen and you can't even comb your own hair. What if a suitor comes to call? You should at least appear presentable."

Mother yanked back my bushy hair and worked it over with my favorite brush. I'd had it since I was a baby and always loved the vine carvings on the handle.

"I shall tie it up." I paused to swallow a bit of crust. "And I don't want a suitor, even if one happened to wander into the hills."

Mother did not reply. I winced and yelped quietly as she pulled and twisted my hair, determined to produce a miracle. She captured two tight braids and secured them atop my head. Not a strand of hair strayed out of place, but the cool air tickled my bare nape.

"There." She set her eyes on mine. "Beautiful. You can wear a brown sack if you choose, but your face Jaclyn, is a thing of beauty. You've got regular features, thank goodness, nothing like your father's crooked nose. And if I did not know you, I'd swear you'd

4

painted those lips rosy. I've always said give me a pair of handsome brown eyes over flighty blue any day. You're living proof."

I shrugged away her compliments. "You're my mother. You're supposed to tell me lies to make me feel better." I turned away and bit off a hunk of bread.

"Nonsense."

Mother huffed and tended to the pot hanging over the fire. Stone by stone, Father had built the fireplace many years past.

I rose. "Shall I help you?"

"Nay, finish your meal. Father awaits." She stirred the previous night's stew with a long wooden spoon.

I sat back down and ran my finger along the ridges of the wooden table, also Father's handiwork. "When will we visit town? I miss the market."

I swallowed my milk after finishing the delicious bread. I wanted to ask for more, but with winter approaching, I kept my lips sealed.

Mother picked up a spoon from a washbasin and wiped it on the fabric around her thin waist. "Do not change the subject of our talk."

"I am not, Mother." I frowned and stood next to her as she dried another spoon.

Mother crinkled her nose. "Don't fret. You're of marriageable age now. We must think of finding you a husband or your time will pass. I'm only thinking of your future, Jaclyn. I want to see you settled soon. Your father and I are not getting younger."

"Getting married and bearing children is not for me. There's much work to be done."

5

I slipped my arms around her waist and pressed my head to her back. I inhaled deeply as warmth enveloped me and her love replaced the fright from my nightmares.

Safe. I am safe. No monsters.

"Our life is good here. Why would I want to fix what is not broken?"

"'Tis what we do. People will talk."

"Let them."

I scowled, anger boiling through my veins. I tended to not raise my voice, so I softened my tone out of respect.

"I will not be handed to a suitor I do not love."

Mother patted my arm. "My child, you have much to learn. Love comes later. I did not love your father at first."

"I will not follow other people's ways." Pouting, I shuffled my feet on the dirt.

She released a deep sigh. "Oh, Jaclyn. Your time will come. Everyone has a destiny. Everyone has a story to tell. Some more than others. We shall see what lies ahead for you. Fate will lead you to the path you are meant to take."

I wished I had eyes for the future. I wanted to know a demon would not seize my soul, and I wanted to see a path without the nighttime cries. They must be monsters. I'd never heard a human throat make such tortured sounds.

What fate awaits a girl who hears monsters at night?

Illness swept through my stomach. A shudder racked me, beginning in my gut, forewarning me.

Chapter Two
Training With Father

"gain." Father waved a wooden sword longer than my arm. "You hit like a girl. Strike harder."

"I am a girl. You wish I were a boy?"

I lunged forward. My boots skidded on the dirt, raising a fine dust. With all my strength, I parried Father's sword when he came at me.

"Nay, child."

The blow knocked Father's arm aside, like many times before, but I had never disarmed him completely. He not only outweighed me, but also stood a head taller.

"Again. Unless you need the rest. Ready to surrender?"

"Never."

I lifted my chin and gripped my sword with determination. The apple tree Father stood under distracted me as thoughts of apple pie, applesauce, and apple spice tea danced through my head.

Father's lips curled down. "You mustn't daze, Jaclyn."

"Aye." I scolded myself and continued to focus.

I struck at him at least twenty times, and twenty times his sword blocked mine. I'd long since stopped counting when stones settled on my chest and I labored to breathe. My arms ached from the force of the collision, but my legs rooted strong beneath me.

The sun provided little warmth in the autumn chill, but the training left me sweaty. The cool air, which had stung minutes before, now felt refreshing.

"My turn." Father's brown eyes darkened. He snarled like a wild animal and came for me.

His bared teeth and fierce scowl, meant to scare me, but made me want to chuckle instead. I dared not. It would not be a laughing matter if I slipped or lost my guard. A blow from his wooden sword would leave me aching for a week.

Father would never willfully hurt me, but he would expect more after a year of practice. He knew precisely my skill level. He declared once he would challenge me until I became his equal, or better.

When his sword met mine, the vibration traveled up my arm, spread through me, and rattled my bones. He held nothing back that day. Father's lips hinted at a smile, a first during sword practice.

"Are you ready for more, Jaclyn?" Father asked, catching his breath.

My heart raced and sweat beaded on my forehead. Angling my sword across my body with the confidence of a knight, I pressed one leg back against the earth to anchor me.

"The question is, Father, are you ready for me?"

Father lifted his eyebrows, surprised by my confidence. He nodded with pride. To another father, my words would have sounded disrespectful, but Father and I had a special bond.

"After a year of training, I hope not. You can outwit this old fool. Being smaller doesn't mean you can't hurt me. Use your entire body and not just the strength of your arm. You haven't much to speak of, after all." He winked.

When Father's sword flew up, I blocked the blow by tilting mine across my body. Loud, warrior yells escaped my mouth as I charged. Then Father pulled back and aimed at my waist. I jumped back, escaping by a hair.

He blocked my advance with his sword and almost knocked mine from my hands. Pulling back, Father aimed below my knees. I leapt over the blade, twirled, and thumped him on the head with the hilt of the sword. Stumbling back, Father smiled.

"You've been secretly training with someone else, eh?" He chuckled, rubbing his head.

He knew it could not be true. No one lived around for miles. It had just been the three of us for as long as I recalled. We used to have visitors and helpers, but they had stopped coming years before. I never asked why, for I liked being isolated from idle gossip and foolish people.

"Nay. You're aging and slower."

He glared at me. "You're not to get arrogant, little one."

I pivoted sideways to dodge his sword, and just before he could regain his stance, I swept his legs and dropped him. It was the first time I'd bested him with wit and strength. Jumping, I howled like a hound. Unladylike, but my training had not been ladylike in any way.

Father stood, looking dazed, and dusted the dirt and loose grass off his tunic. "Well, I did not expect that. I reckon you need a greater challenge."

I stiffened.

"I will not hold anything back, you hear? Keep your eyes fixed. Let this be a warning, my child."

I swallowed a mouthful of fear. "Ready."

Meeting his gaze, I brought my sword up and flexed my fingers, then tightened my grip with anticipation.

Father charged, swinging.

Every impact jarred my arms painfully until I thought my bones might shatter. The little triumph I had fled. I struggled with each slash of my wooden sword to meet Father's agile moves. With every miss, it took me longer to recover, and his lightning-fast swings battered me.

As he swung and I blocked, we moved across the field. I stepped on a branch, lost my footing and stumbled. A couple of times, I tripped while evading his sword. When a pebble rolled underfoot, I twisted my ankle.

Each fall made my muscles grow heavier. After countless minutes had passed, I was spent.

"Ready to cease?" Father slowed. Though he tried not to show his exhaustion, his heavy breathing betrayed him.

"Nay." I panted.

My throat scratched like grains of sand rubbing together, and my tunic clung to my back. Sweat trickled down my cheeks, and loose strands of hair stuck to my face.

Father lowered his sword, tip pointing toward the ground, and wiped the sweat from his forehead with the hem of his tunic.

"Good. That's what I want to hear. If they come from all sides, you'll not have time to rest. Kill or be killed. You must open your eyes always."

"Is war coming?"

Father's eyes widened. "Nay. Who told you a false tale?"

"No one. I assumed from the training."

"No man or woman should feel helpless. I want to ensure you can defend yourself in a time of need. I will not always be around."

I frowned. "Nay, Father. You'll grow old with me."

Father's lips twitched with a hint of a smile, I hoped from his approval of my words.

"My time will pass, but hopefully not too soon."

Father's talk of death pierced my heart. Mother told stories of the Black Death that had taken so many lives over a hundred and fifty years before. Struck with fever, the sick had raved as though they had seen demons. Swelling had appeared in soft places, hard and burning, and then victims had vomited blood. I imagined the suffering, a horrid way to die.

Perhaps the cries I heard in my waking nightmares were the sounds of those poor souls.

I swiped at tall grasses with my sword, for I did not want to imagine these people or my life without Father and Mother.

"Would you like to rest?" Father brought me back to the present.

"Aye."

I dropped my arms to my sides. The sword grew heavy as a tree, and my arm muscles throbbed. I should be used to holding my weapon for so long, but no matter the months of training, Father always pushed me just past my limit. The thrill of battle spurred me on when practicing with him, but would I be able to endure in real life?

11

Father rested his hand on my back, guiding me as we strode toward our cozy house. Mother would be bustling about the kitchen and, with luck, a hearty midday meal would be waiting in the common room.

As we neared the house, cows and sheep greeted us from their paddocks. Tom, the fine calico mouser, darted into the barn, doubtlessly chasing some vermin in the hay we'd laid in for winter. I noted the autumn bounty waiting for harvest in the garden. The vegetables and apples from the trees we'd practiced under would make some of my chores in coming weeks.

The gloomy clouds had bunched together. Their ominous bellies thickened, thrumming with charged energy. Far off in the distance, more storm clouds, black as the devil's heart, headed toward us. Rain would surely come our way. The cool breeze that had been a relief earlier stung through the fabrics, making me shiver.

As we neared our house, Mother greeted us. She had taken off the cotton square from around her waist to reveal a simple lavender dress. Mother frowned when she eyed my destroyed braided bun and again when she saw the dirt on my clothes. She gave me a cup of water and then shifted her attention to Father.

"Richard." Mother placed a hand on Father's arm. "You almost killed our daughter. She's just a girl, not a boy."

Her comment struck me. Had Father always wanted a boy instead? He loved me, but I secretly wished I were a boy for him. Perhaps I would be a better fighting companion.

Mother turned to me. "You didn't get hurt, did you?"

She took the empty cup from me, handed it to Father, and

then took my wooden sword, relieving the pressure on my shoulder.

"Thank you for the water, Mother." I already wanted more. "And I'm well, I assure you. No need to scold Father."

I lagged behind, annoyed, as we continued toward the house. I wished she would stop fussing over me. Many girls my age had already wed or gone into service with a wealthy family. Just because I hadn't left home did not mean she should treat me like a child.

Mother should have been used to my training. I had been training with Father since I was old enough to hold a weapon, though I understood her concern. Father had used more force that day, and my garments and hair likely showed it. He had fought me as if we were on equal ground.

I felt proud, and my confidence grew.

"Midday meal is ready."

Her lips became a thin line, and I sensed a change in her attitude. She mustn't be pleased with my tone.

"Thank you, Mother. My tummy eagerly awaits the delicious food," I said to appease her.

I hadn't meant to sound ungrateful—she was only thinking of my well-being—but the hunger pangs and exhaustion had put me in an ill mood.

Mother's face softened, and her lips tugged at the corner. "Thank you, Jaclyn. I made your favorite soup."

"I can't wait to eat it, but before I do, may I visit Angel? I woke late this morning and didn't have a chance to greet her."

"Be quick about it," Mother said. "If you don't hurry, your

soup will get cold."

"You're the best mother in all the land."

"I'm your *only* mother." A soft giggle escaped her mouth.

"But you're still the best."

I gave her an innocent smile she could not resist and then sprinted away.

Chapter Three
Hidden Hoard

The sun glowed through the small barn windows high above like Heaven's light. Fresh hay and earthy horse dung, the scents of home, swirled around me as my shuffling caused a stir among the livestock.

The chickens quickened their steps and scattered, giving me a clear path. I waved my arms like Moses parting the water. My father's horse, Daniel, turned his head toward me, then Angel did the same.

Angel stepped forward and stood in the sunlight. With a coat white as snow, she looked majestic. I'd chosen her name. Angel. She looked like one with the sun's rays pouring down on her in glowing ribbons. All she needed was a set of wings.

Father had traded for her at a nearby town the year before. She'd cost two gold coins and a bushel of apples. I had never seen such rare beauty before.

Angel's tail flopped back and forth, her head bobbing in recognition as I came for her. Tied up, she could not move any more than the length the rope allowed.

"Good day, Angel." I stroked along her smooth back as I nestled my head by the side of her neck.

She nickered in response. Backing away, I examined her body.

"I had a terrible dream again."

I swept the barn with my eyes. I needn't, as the nearest home lay miles away.

"You don't think I'm turning into a demon, do you?" I released a heavy breath. "I suppose I'm a lackwit for asking such a question. But the cries frighten me. These dreams have come almost every fortnight since I turned sixteen. I feel like the devil is coming for me or perhaps I'm turning into … I've gone mad, I tell you." I shook my head and let out a soft laugh. "I train with Father each day. I'm getting faster and stronger. I hope never to raise my sword, in truth, but 'tis better to be prepared."

Angel bobbed her head and puffed air from her nose. She might not be able to speak, but she understood me.

"I must get back. Midday meal awaits."

Instead, I jumped to sit on the bale of hay. Being with Angel always gave me a sense of serenity, and talking to her helped me push the previous night's terror aside. As my feet dangled, I grabbed a piece of hay and stuck it in my mouth.

"Does it taste good, Angel?" I laughed as I chewed.

With no one aside from my parents to confide in, I found comfort in talking to Angel.

Angel's mouth opened to grab the end of the piece, so I let her have it. I didn't relish the taste of dried grass, anyway.

Peering up to the high ceiling, I marveled at the craftsmanship of the structure Father and his friends had built. All the boards angled up to an arch in the middle. In the center, spider webs hung in intricate patterns of fine artistry, glistening in the sunlight.

"Jaclyn."

Mother's voice carried on the wind. I flinched and sprang down.

"Well, Mother calls, Angel. I'll visit after chores."

I caressed her once more. On my way out, I stopped by Daniel's stall. He came toward me, and I rubbed his head.

"Greetings, Daniel. Look after Angel for me, eh?"

Father had taught me the first rule of caring for horses was to examine their bodies for cuts and bruises. He had been there that morning, but I checked Daniel anyway. As I studied Daniel, something shiny reflected a blinding gleam in my eyes.

I took a step back, blinking, then leaned forward, hoping I would catch it again. When nothing happened, I looked over my shoulder, making sure Father did not lurk, and went inside Daniel's stall.

"Good day, Daniel." I ran my hand the length of his body.

I invaded his domain with care, unsure what he would do. Daniel ignored me and let me slide by. Bending to my knees, I shuffled the hay and dirt away.

What in Heaven's name?

The wooden boards lay side by side but had enough space between them for the light to penetrate if the sun hit the right spot. A hidden secret hoard lay below the straw.

My imagination ran wild. What if I had found gold? But Father had built the place, so he would have known about it.

Then, perhaps, he'd stored gold there for desperate times. Whatever lay inside, he mustn't wish me to see.

No, Jaclyn, don't look. Don't do it.

But why not? Don't you want to know?

17

Curiosity won, and I needed to find out.

My heart pounded as I gripped the handle and lifted. A black, threadbare blanket covered the items inside, but a tip of something stuck out. The tip must have been what caught the light, but it did not seem shiny enough.

It did not matter what had caught my attention; fate had brought me to find what was inside the hoard. Or so I told myself to justify acting like a thief.

Unfolding the cloth to the left and then right revealed the hidden objects. A sword, two daggers, and one old lance rested inside.

The beautiful sword had been made of fine, polished steel with an intricate design crafted into the handle. It looked like a sword the king's soldiers would use.

I wanted to hold it, but I dared not. I needed to leave. Mother or Father would come looking for me.

Against my better judgment, I reached for the lance.

It did not appear to be anything special—not valuable like the sword. Why would Father hide an old lance as if it were some sort of treasure?

I began to tug out the lance, careful not to poke Daniel or the wooden walls in such a tight cramped space. Taking a step away from the poop and shifting my body every which way possible, I pulled the lance out, avoiding Daniel's hooves.

Surprisingly light in my hands, the aged but smooth rod felt cold, like an icicle on a winter branch. The tip had been made of steel—simple, yet a golden streak curled upward to the point.

Real gold? Brass, perhaps.

I studied it, intrigued as to why Father had it and where he had found it. Placed upright, it towered over me. I could not question him unless I admitted sneaking, and I did not think he would like his daughter poking around where she did not belong.

"Jaclyn?"

Father.

I needed to go.

Yet, the lance captivated me enough to pay the price of Father catching me red-handed. Running my finger along the length once more, I decided to test its sharpness.

"Jaclyn."

Father's voice echoed from outside the barn.

Just as I touched the tip, it nicked me. I gasped and jerked back, not by the cut, but from the sensation. I felt as if I'd touched a boiling pot. Heat blazed through me, something strange happened when I got that wound. I saw an image.

Something with amber eyes had stared at me, but I didn't understand what I'd seen. Was it the devil? It flashed for a split second, but faded just as I dropped the lance.

Oh, Lord.

I shuddered and rubbed my arms.

The lance clattering to the barn floor startled Daniel. He began to stamp and shift in the small space, making a lot of noise.

Stupid horse.

It took a great deal of care to grab the lance without getting kicked.

No, not stupid horse, stupid me.

I scrambled to put it back. Then I covered everything with the

19

blanket the way it had been, closed the lid, and shuffled back the hay and dirt. Wincing, I sucked the small pearl of blood on my fingertip, covering any evidence of what had happened.

"Jaclyn, are you here?"

My heart galloped faster. I slapped my arms behind me, hoping Father would not suspect anything.

"Father. I'm here with Daniel."

Pressing my back against the wall, I shifted away from Daniel. My heart hammered in my ears as I covered them to drown out Daniel's agitated snorts.

Father's pounding footsteps came closer, and then he appeared. He stroked Daniel to calm him down.

"Whoa, Daniel. All is well." As he continued to caress Daniel, he shifted his attention to me. "Jaclyn. Why are you in here?" He spoke softly to soothe the horse, but his eyes showed anger.

I stilled, afraid to move. Any disturbance would spook Daniel again. I had to think fast. Easy enough. I had become a great storyteller from the lack of playmates. Since childhood, I'd spun tales to entertain my parents after dinner.

"I thought I saw a cut in his hind leg, so I decided to examine him. I wanted to make you proud of me." I lowered my arms to my sides and smiled sheepishly.

His irate expression relaxed. "I already checked him this morning. He's well. Go eat your meal."

"I will."

Step by step, I carefully moved around Daniel.

When Father turned away, I rubbed at my index finger. I had only touched the tip of the lance, not pressed my finger into it.

How had it nicked me?

Perhaps my imagination had captured me. Mayhap the stories I made up addled my mind.

I gazed at my fingertip again and found no hint of a cut, only a smudge of blood I had wiped away. After rubbing my eyes, I looked again.

Nothing.

I blinked and looked again.

No cut?

I stared and stared.

Impossible.

I shook my head and blamed it on lack of sleep, but it didn't explain the blood.

Before I left, I looked over my shoulder at Angel. She would not have been startled like Daniel. Angel would have remained silent and still.

Standing under the sun's rays as if she enjoyed the warmth, she appeared tranquil as could be.

My beautiful angel without wings.

Chapter Four
The Story

hen day neared the end, the sun settled low across the horizon, casting hues of fiery red and orange. As Mother made supper, Father and I tended to the animals.

Sweat dampened my forehead and rolled down my back under the loose tunic. Dirt smeared my face, hands, and clothes, and I stank like the pigs.

Father took off his hat, wiped the sweat from his forehead, and placed his hat back on his head as we continued toward the house. Day after day, he wore the same ridiculous hat.

"Your hat is old and ragged. I shall buy you a new one."

Father dipped his head low, catching his hat in his hand, and stuck a finger through the hole on the top. He inhaled a deep breath, seemed to search for words, but kept quiet.

"This hat holds a special place in my heart," he finally said. "I've had it since the day you blessed my life. It holds a wonderful memory of you. I shall hold it forever and carry it with me wherever I go, as I carry you in my heart always. I do not need a new hat. It has flaws, but 'tis mostly whole and still useful."

My heart soared and filled with happiness. Father rarely spoke so tenderly, but when he did, he lifted my spirits and gave me wings to fly.

I wanted to tell him I loved him, though we hardly spoke those words. Father showed his love through actions. Actions carried more weight, anyway.

Though it would have been nice to hear the sentiment from him, or to say it myself.

"Why not ask Mother to patch it?"

Mother spent countless hours mending holes in our tunics. Never waste what can be fixed, she'd say.

"It would not be the same. The hat shows what it endured. If you can forgive its flaws and see the beauty, then it is saved. Keep my words to heart, Jaclyn. Forgive and show love. Lead with love in your heart. Then you shall shine through the deepest darkness. That is the way to save and to be saved."

"Aye."

Father no longer meant the hat. He often taught me lessons from commonplace things. But that lesson he gave so often, I could repeat it in my sleep.

"Who shall wash first?" Father dusted the dirt off his tunic.

"Draw straws for it?"

Father smirked, and he stopped to pluck two weeds growing by the house. "Which of these will you choose?"

He arranged the stems in his hand and held them out to me. When I drew one, he declared it the long straw and dropped his own. I pretended not to notice his was longer. Instead, I jumped for joy.

"I won."

Father's smile glowed. With his permission, I skipped to the back of the house. As always, Mother had fetched a bucket of water for us to wash in.

After dipping the rag, I twisted it to squeeze the icy water and wiped my face. It stung my bones as I washed under my garments and along my hairline. Then I changed into fresh clothing in my chamber.

Father came inside just as the silhouette of the thick dark clouds in the night sky appeared. No rain had fallen, but I sensed it would soon.

Mother had set candles to light our cozy home, and a fire crackled under the cooking pot to keep us warm. The smell of Mother's stew drew growls from my stomach as I helped her ready supper.

"Say grace, Jaclyn." Father set his elbows on the table, hands clasped, and lowered his head.

He had never asked me to pray before a meal, so his request surprised me.

"Grace." I giggled.

I loved teasing Father. His eyebrows furrowed as if I had spoken in a different tongue. Then he chuckled softly when he caught on to my childish jest.

"Jaclyn." Mother wagged her finger.

I snickered under my breath.

"Pray," Father requested again, narrowing his eyes at me with a hint of a smile. Despite his stern tone, his lips kept twitching.

"Aye." Clasping my hands, I bowed my head and closed my eyes. "Heavenly Father, I thank thee for a good day and for our meal we're about to receive. Please forgive our sins"—I thought about the snooping I'd done in the barn earlier—"and deliver us from evil." When I opened my eyes, my parents nodded with approval.

Mother poured stew into a wooden trencher before me, and then she passed fresh bread while Father placed a chicken leg on my plate. My mouth watered at the rare treat. After I poured the milk into our cups, we were set to eat.

"I shall be going to town the day after tomorrow." Father scooped stew into his mouth and pulled a piece from his chunk of bread. "It'll be just you and your mother. I'm entrusting you with a sword. You will be fine. I'm sure of it, like many times I've been away before. I've trained you well."

"Yes, Father." I swallowed a piece of meat I hadn't chewed well enough, surprised at Father's unexpected news. "How long will you be in town?"

"Just a day. But it will be a day's travel to reach town and another to return home." He took a sip of his drink.

Mother smiled at Father, her eyes gleaming in the firelight. "We'll be fine. Don't you worry about us. Jaclyn, you didn't know, but I'm skilled with a sword myself. Who do you think trained your father?"

I spat milk out of my mouth. I covered my lips with my hands in shock at Mother's teasing and horror for what I'd done.

"I'm so sorry," I mumbled against my palms.

The look on Father's face made me laugh aloud. His pride was plentiful enough to fill the room, and for Mother to belittle him— there were no words for his disgruntled scowl. Mother went to get a cloth to wipe up my mess, and Father roared with laughter.

"Your mother is right. She taught me everything I know." He winked and then bestowed upon her a charming leer.

Grace of God.

Moments like that, I turned away and pretended not to know.

My parents occasionally stole a quick kiss in front of me, but when they shared intimate moments, thinking I would not notice, it turned my stomach. The thought of them doing what was natural—enjoying the marital pleasures between a husband and wife—made me want to live in a house of my own. But children lived with their parents until they were wed. With no suitors and none likely to appear, I would live with my parents, no doubt, for the rest of my life.

After supper, I sat by the fire. With a blanket keeping me warm, I drank hot apple tea Mother had made with fresh apples. She'd added some spices, making it sweet and delicious.

Some nights Father would read the Bible, or I would sing songs. Other nights, I would entertain them with my tales.

Father cleared his throat. "Since we read the Bible last night, Jaclyn, would you like to share a story, or shall you retire to your chamber?"

"Indeed, I have one in mind." My heart leaped for joy and I wrapped my fingers around the cup for warmth.

"Let us hear it." Mother adjusted her blanket higher to her waist.

My mind wandered to the barn, recalling the lance. "There once lived a girl, fair and innocent. Her hair flowed like golden silk and skin was soft as rose petals. She lived in a town with her sister and her parents."

My parents smiled, their eyes eager.

"One night, monsters invaded the town. Skilled with weaponry, taught by her father, she slayed the monsters." I swung my arm as if I held a sword and dropped my voice lower. "But even still, night after night, the monsters came." I paused for dramatic effect. "Then one day, the girl dreamt of a special weapon, hidden nearby. She searched the town for the lance—a lance made of pure gold." I recalled the golden streak snaking up the lance's long point. "When she found it in a church, she told the priest about her dream. The priest let her take it without further questioning, for he had heard of a legend that a girl would save the people."

I took a sip of my tea and continued as I watched my parents' stunned expressions. "When the monsters came back, the girl slayed the master of the monsters with her lance. When the master died, all the monsters ignited in flames and burned in Hell. The king paid her for her service, and their family lived wealthy and well. The end."

Throughout the story, I had kept my attention mostly on Father, who seemed fascinated at first, but then his expression changed to alarm. He'd frowned when I mentioned the lance.

Had I said words to offend? Surely he would not know I had found his secret weapons. My parents normally clapped and told me I had an imaginative mind, but no praise escaped their lips.

"Did my story not entertain you?" I asked, baffled.

I'd told a different tale than the usual ones of girls who go to castles and meet princes. I thought Father would enjoy hearing one in which the father trained his daughter, who put the skills to good use.

Father blinked and stood in haste. He tried not to show his disapproval, but his forehead creased, and his jaw clenched. "I thought it ... entertaining. I'm overtired this night. Don't delay your sleep. Early morning chores await." He stretched to yawn after changing the subject.

"'Tis late. Sleep well." Mother did not pay me any compliment, and gathered each end to fold the blankets.

My heart sank to my feet. I nodded, picked up a lantern, and paced to my chamber with my head down and shoulders slumped.

I shall never repeat such a tiresome story again.

"Say your prayers, Jaclyn." Father's voice muffled through the closed door.

"Aye, Father." The words came out sluggish and disappointed.

I pondered again why no praises had been given. I'd thought it a clever tale. When I heard whispers, I pressed my ear to the door.

"Richard," Mother began. "You mustn't ... lance..."

Lance? What about it?

"Shall not ... worry..." Father muttered.

Mother is worried. Why?

I pulled away when their words faded to murmurs and I socked the door out of frustration. Pain shot to my bone. I tried to rub the soreness away.

Stupid thick door.

After I placed the lantern next to my bed, I undressed and gently brushed my finger over my birthmarks.

Small, dark circles stained the middle of each wrist and on my feet at the places where the nails had pierced Jesus on the cross. When I had asked my parents about such strangeness, they'd told me the spots were birthmarks, of which I should not be ashamed, but some people could believe me to be a witch or a miracle.

They feared either the church or the meddling neighbors might take me away. I had been told not to show or speak of my marks around others.

People fear what they do not understand.

I blew out the candle inside the lantern and slid into bed after dressing in my thick chemise. Shivering, I hugged the covers.

My mind drifted to the lance, recalling how it had pricked me, and the flash of something unexplainable that followed it. Whatever it had been, there wasn't anything angelic about it. Maybe the devil had showed himself to me.

Rage and pain had gutted me during the brief vision. The image and the feeling haunted me. Something extraordinary had happened. I sensed it in my deepest soul.

I wished I knew what it meant. Perhaps nothing at all, but the possibility it could be the devil's work did not sit well. Before I attempted to gather my thoughts to pray, my exhausted body and mind found sleep.

Chapter Five

Monsters Are Real

y eyes flashed open and I folded my arms. A murky vision of a demon with teeth like knives and blood-red eyes had disturbed my sleep.

The monster tale I'd told haunted me. I must never speak of it again. Trembling, I told myself I was safe and released a sigh of relief.

Darkness blanketed my room. How long had I been asleep?

Lying silently, I listened to the leaves fluttering in the strong breeze. Peace filled the night until thunder boomed. I jerked and gasped in fright. Then my stomach growled in hunger.

I debated whether to fetch cold stew from the pot, but when the urge to relieve myself came strong, I had only one choice.

Cursing under my breath, I shoved my feet into my boots and wrapped the coverlet around me. Feeling my way out of my room, thankful for the embers' lingering light, I made my way out the front door with my lantern.

The crisp, icy wind slapped my face and prickled under my skin. I quickened my steps to the back of the house, but the chilly breeze and the muddy soil from the earlier rain made it difficult. I almost slipped several times from the mushy mud.

After I did my business, I sprinted toward the front, but a

flickering light caught my eye from the barn. My parents were asleep in their chamber. So who dared to linger in the middle of night?

I should have awakened Father, but curiosity filled my mind when I spotted a dozen horses tied up. The strangers might hear me or leave before I woke Father. I had to know why and who was there.

No, no, no, Jaclyn. Don't be a fool. It may be dangerous.

Just a quick peek and I would leave. Curiosity always won over the possibility of being scolded.

The light brightened and the whispers grew louder as I approached. I settled by a crack near the side of the barn. Tucking my knees to my chest as I lowered to the ground, I shielded my head with my coverlet and huddled to keep warm as I peeked through the hole.

A dozen lanterns formed a circle, flooding the area in a golden glow around a group of men. I gasped at the sight of my father standing among them, leaning against Daniel's stable door. Some stood and some sat on bales of hay. Most of the men were my father's age, but several looked younger.

The men dressed alike—dark tunics, pants tucked in boots, and thick, black capes. Hats blocked some of their faces. I did not recognize any of them, but we hardly had any visitors.

Why would Father hold a gathering there and so late into the night? Were they going hunting? He would have told me. Perhaps they were planning a trip to town together?

"The danger grows worse. Our flocks have dwindled. We must find the predator taking our sheep," a red-headed man with a round belly hanging over his trousers said.

"Mayhap you lost them?" One snorted. "They run faster than you. Or mayhap you ate them and don't remember. Your belly is showing your guilt."

Chuckles filled the air, but Father cut it short by raising his hand.

"'Tis not the time to laugh. Aldwin is right. People all over the shire say the same. We must find the reason."

A tall man, built like my father, stepped forward. He had his back turned to me, so I could not see his face, but when he slightly angled his head I saw he had a beard.

"I know the answer, but you won't believe me."

His tone declared confidence, but I detected a note of fear.

Another man stepped forward. "I might know what thief steals our sheep, but it's ... it's ..."

With dark hair and green eyes, he looked familiar. When he craned his neck, I got a better view of him. Jack's father.

Jack was a year older than me. Our families used to meet for gatherings in my younger days, but I hadn't seen him in two years or so.

"Speak, William. It's all right," my father said.

A long stretch of silence filled the air. The men became still and quiet, leaning closer with anticipation on their faces. Blowing breath on my hands, I too waited.

William gathered his cape tighter. "We've all heard of the night monsters. If you have not, let me enlighten you." He paused and gazed at each man. When no one stopped him, he continued, "It is said the horrendous sounds first vibrated through the villages near Black Mountain about sixteen years ago. I—"

"I've never heard of such a place. Where is this Black Mountain?" A young one adjusted his hat and scratched the back of his head.

William furrowed his brow and glared at him. I would too for interrupting. But William continued to be a noble man.

"It's almost a day's travel from here, past the market town, Hampton, and past the thieves' forest most people fear. As I was saying, the torturous sounds filled the night, often three times or more within a month. Tales are abundant, but not a single soul knew for sure the reason. No one in memory dared to venture or examine the truthfulness of the tales, even with the promise of treasures beyond imagination up on Black Mountain."

"Treasure?" The man sitting on bales of hay leaned closer.

The man with dark curly hair licked his lips hungrily. "What kind of treasures?"

William held up a hand. "It's not worth the risk of our lives, Peter."

"Gold?" a man who hadn't spoken until that moment asked.

"Treasures of gold and silver and jewels beyond imagination are said to be hidden in the cavern. But those are only a tale," William said. "There is no proof."

"What do these monsters look like?" another one asked, shuffling his feet.

"Perhaps they are humans possessed by demons?" one said.

"They say the night monsters are taller than life, have claws like a beast, and teeth as sharp as knives. They thirst for blood and kill for sport. Some say they look half-human and half-beast, an

33

abomination of God's creation," William answered, his voice thick and low.

Eerie chills ran up my spine, and my heart drummed mercilessly. I looked over my shoulder, making sure no such monster crawled behind me. But when William mentioned the torturous sounds filling the night, at least three times or more within a month, I'd lost my breath and clutched my blanket tighter.

Surely there was no connection to the sounds I'd heard in my dreams. William had admitted his tales were merely legends, and the sounds were in my head. No one else heard them. They were just ... What could they be?

The man whose face I could not see laughed. "These are all lies. We've all heard tales of werewolves and vampires. There are no such creatures. Tales are just tales, to keep the young from going out late at night. My parents used to tell me the same tales."

The argument exploded.

When Father raised his hand, I expected everyone to stop, but the men involved in the heated conversation ignored him. Father whistled between his teeth. Daniel and Angel snapped their heads up. Then Father finally caught the men's attention.

"You may think it only a tale, but some of us know the story isn't just a tale. It is real."

I gasped and then shoved my fist to my mouth to keep silent.

More voices erupted.

Father raised his hand again. "Please, allow me to continue, and then you may decide." He waited until everyone settled. "Some of you are too young to recall, but the night monsters were the reason people from Riverway, Woodmont, and Forestway—the villages once closest to Black Mountain—moved away. I did not know of such demons when I built our home. It seemed like the perfect place. A clear stream flowed nearby. The land was green and trees plenty. If I thought it odd so few villages were in this area, I thought only God had provided. And the king thought the same. That was one reason he asked William and me to look after the land and the people near Black Mountain."

"Lies," the young one with blond hair accused. "Why would the king excuse you from service in his army while so young?"

Father frowned and tightened a fist like he wanted to punch the youngling. "William and I fought bravely in many battles, long before you were born. The king gave us land and excused us of our duty. We were to live there and keep watch over the villages in his name, and that is all you need to know." Father looked upon William with sadness in his eyes.

Father had fought for the king?

It was how he'd gained such skill with a sword. I'd learned so much about Father in a few minutes. What else has he not told?

William nodded, as if they had some sort of unspoken exchange of thoughts, and then began to speak.

"Richard spoke truly. We once lived in the same town, though we were not as close to the mountain as the other villages." He jerked his head toward a man standing on the right. "And so did John."

"Aye," John said.

"All was well." William's green eyes dazed as if he could see the monsters from the years past. "Until ... one night, a year or more

35

after I arrived, demonic screams echoed into the mountains and traveled to our homes. They disturbed my sleep and filled me with terror. I imagined the worst: people suffering, their limbs being ripped apart, and being eaten alive. And the rumors I'd heard from other villages came true."

I shivered and pressed my hands to my forehead. Twisting grimaces marked each of the men's faces, at least the ones I could see.

Father cleared his throat. "Indeed they did. When I visited the other towns closest to Black Mountain to trade, I learned something had been preying on their sheep. People from those towns claimed friends had also gone missing. They described the monsters just as William told you. And eventually, they moved elsewhere. Soon after, all the towns nearest to Black Mountain became desolate. We were the only town left. And just as William described, we too began to hear the cries. We could bear it no more. We scattered away from Black Mountain."

The stocky, red-headed man named Aldwin, rubbed his throat. "I do not believe this man who claims to have seen such abominations. There are no such things. I believe it to be men possessed by the devil."

A man sitting on the hay stood as he spoke, pointing a challenging stare at Father. "I lived in that same town, William, but I recall Richard leaving before his daughter was born."

Father stood taller, returning a bold and unyielding gaze. "I left for other reasons I do not wish to share. I fled with my family when everyone else did. But I did not go far. The town business was my business. My group of men kept everyone safe during the journey to new homes. I wish not to be mocked."

The man shrank back.

Father had never told me about when he and Mother lived in town. He'd never discussed the events of his life before I was born, or even soon after. The only life I'd known was our home, isolated from everyone else.

I understood why we had moved now. I had thought we lived so far from people only to hide my birthmarks as long as possible. It seemed natural to have such thoughts when we did not attend church like other families. Instead the priest came to our home, and we rarely went to town …

No, *I* rarely went to town.

The thought of moving away because of night monsters—ones Father claimed to be real—was a shock to my soul. I pressed closer to the wall, straining to hear the men.

"What is our plan?" Aldwin's jaw clenched. "We can't let them take our sheep, be they monsters or possessed men. What will happen next? The cows, pigs, and then we are next. Perhaps they've already taken people."

"We must kill it." A man raised a fist.

"Nay." The wrinkle on Father's forehead creased deeper. "If they are truly men, even men possessed, we cannot kill them. How can we think ourselves made in the likeness of God when we act worse than beasts? I want to see for myself. I'm going to bring a few of my sheep. I'll meet you at my old town in three days, where the church once was. We'll use my sheep as bait. We'll keep a watch until it comes for them."

"You've gone mad," a young man with a stocking hat said.

"It's the only way to lure one out, unless you want to go to the mountain yourself." William arched his eyebrows.

"You want to capture one? The demon speaks through your mouth," the same fellow retorted. "I say we kill them all."

"We do not kill." My father gritted his teeth.

His determined eyes flickered back away from the lantern. With a clenched jaw and fists rounded, he stepped toward the speaker.

"If you're not at ease with this, then do not show yourselves. I've gathered this group to keep our homes and livelihoods safe against whatever may threaten it. Some of us have fought battles together for the king. We are brothers, family. We are all we have. Perhaps after we settle all this, my family shall join some of you in a village. I miss your fellowship."

"Me too." John nodded curtly.

"And I." William looked at my father with brotherly affection.

A few more agreed.

"What shall we do if we capture these creatures or madmen?" Peter rubbed his dark, curly hair.

Father crossed his arms and sighed. "I do not plan to capture it. I want to see with my own eyes. I believe it to be monsters. Whatever caused us to move, to fear, we need to clear this matter. The problem is spreading."

"I agree." William scrubbed his face. "We cannot fight the devil. We will not win."

"I second." John scratched under his chin.

Some of the other men agreed, but others kept quiet.

"Sun will arise soon. The wives will know we're missing."

Aldwin retrieved a sword from the ground and stood.

When William let go of his cape, his sword caught my eyes. It resembled the one Father had hidden away. John and a few others had the same sword, too. Of course, they had all served the king. But for some reason, Father had hidden his special sword away when he left the king's army.

"For those who are willing, I'll see you in three days." Father gave a half-grin and adjusted his hat on his head. "Thank you for coming. Please wipe away the shoe prints as you leave. Have a safe journey back home. Godspeed."

Three days?

Father had mentioned a trip to town in three days. It appeared he had another destination in mind.

The men slapping Father on the shoulder one by one signaled time to leave. That night I heard a side of Father I'd never known. My respect for him rose even greater. He was well known by his former townspeople. He protected them, served them, and cared about them.

The men spoke to Father with reverence, at least the older ones with whom he had a kinship. None of them would have been there late into the night if they hadn't sought his advice.

But the beasts—they were real whether the men believed or not. I believed because Father said they were, and I'd heard their cries for months.

The monsters' wails had first invaded my mind the day I turned sixteen. How many heard their cries at night like me and never told a soul, afraid to be cast out of their village or burned for a heretic?

A silent, deadly chill took hold of every bone and muscle. Small wonder he had not liked my monster tale the previous night.

When father flung the barn door open, I had no time to think but run back home. Who knew what kind of scolding I would receive if I were caught? I had seen no women at the meeting, let alone children.

Water descended in gleaming silver drops from the night sky, a gentle kiss on my face. I tightened my coverlet and ran against the frigid wind as fast as my legs would carry me.

Boots pounded against the wet dirt as the rain poured heavier and thicker on the spongy Earth. My face went numb, and then my body, not just from the savage cold, but from my thoughts.

They are real ... real. Taller than life ... claws like a beast ... teeth as sharp as knives.

I reached home with speed I never knew I had. Panting and desperate for air, I slipped inside quietly and walked with careful steps so as not to disturb Mother. Then I threw my coverlet across the bed and scooted under the damp blanket.

My hammering heart slowed to a steadier beat but refused to calm. I had discovered much through the crack in the wall. Having early chores in the morning, I closed my eyes for sleep, shivering, but sleep would not come.

Thoughts of monsters took hold of my mind.

They are real.

Chapter Six

Monsters In My Wake

The celestial fireball broke through the lingering gray streaks and greeted a sparkling new day after the night's rain, and a scent of wet grass and soil filled the air. I yawned and stretched as the roosters crowed.

After I cleaned the horse stalls and pigpen, I collected the eggs and milked the cow. Then I placed the eggs and a jar of milk on the table so Mother would find them when she awoke. Those chores were hard labor, but I looked forward to spending time with Angel before the morning meal.

Angel shook her head and whipped her tail when I entered. She always stood in a sun-filled spot inside her stall. Glancing to Daniel, I thought about the lance again. Its point drew blood but left no wound.

"What do you suggest I do, Angel?" I stroked her coarse mane. "Shall I peek at the lance once more?"

I had little time to think. Father would appear soon. As I circled where the men had stood the night before, I replayed their words about the monsters and wiped away traces of footprints with my boot.

Please wipe away the shoe prints as you leave, Father had asked. A few men had been careless.

The need to know whether the lance had really cut me possessed my mind. The devil might truly take my soul if I did not learn the truth.

"I'm going to visit Daniel." I grabbed a handful of hay and held it out for Angel. "See, I love you more. I shall be back." Then I grabbed a handful of hay for Daniel, too.

I opened the latch, carefully stepped inside, and stroked Daniel's head. After I fed him some hay, I maneuvered around him. Sinking to my knees, I dusted an area around the handle and pulled it up. The lance lay under the flap of black fabric, in the same position I'd left it.

I slid it out of the floor vault and slipped out of the stall, afraid I might drop it again and startle Daniel. Again, I gently ran my finger along the length, hoping to repeat what I'd done before.

My breath caught in my throat the closer I got to the sharp edge, and my heart raced faster from the anticipation. Then I touched the tip.

Silence.

I slapped my forehead in frustration and touched the tip again. Nothing.

I shook the weapon, angry at the stupid object consuming my waking thoughts. At a loss, I wrapped my hand around it to drag it back in place, but my hand slipped and touched the tip.

I gasped, dropped the lance, and folded my arms around my waist. An image flashed before me—the gruesome monster of the men's tales, with a long, hairy body and glowing amber eyes.

Its yellowed teeth were sharp like knives, and its hands bore claws long and jagged enough to rip a body to shreds. Horrified by the vision, I quivered in fright and my legs weakened.

Taller than life ... claws like a beast ... teeth as sharp as knives.

The devil had possessed me as punishment for sneaking, no doubt.

Daniel did not spook like before, but I was out of my mind. Listening to the men talk about monsters had prepared me for fear. I couldn't bear seeing monsters during my waking hours, too. Even Angel would look like a monster, and I would lose my only friend.

I swore at the lance, placed it back, and then patted Daniel. I thanked him for being silent and walked out of his stall.

At that moment, Father walked in.

I bristled and held my breath.

"Good day. How did you sleep?" Father stood by the door, holding his hat.

His bright brown eyes looked refreshed, ready to start anew, but I, on the other hand, wanted to crawl back into bed.

"As well as can be." I stretched my arms to the ceiling and yawned.

Father arched his brows, but he did not speak a word. His eyes roamed about the floor and shifted toward the direction where Daniel stood.

Could he tell I'd been snooping?

Then he glanced around, perhaps searching for something. He knew I had been the only one there.

"You did well with chores." Father met my gaze again.

When his finger poked through the hole, I frowned at his hat. He should at least have mother mend it or buy a new one.

"Of course I did," I said.

43

He'd never praised me for finishing my chores before. So very strange.

Father took long strides to Daniel, his eyes dancing in the sunlight as he looked about, then cut back to me.

I held my breath, my pulse racing. He knew. I would surely be scolded.

"Everything fine in here?" The corner of his eyes creased when he schooled his face.

I did a turnabout, tilted my head back to glance at the ceiling, and gazed at the same web I admired before. "Nothing new but the spiders." I let out a nervous giggle, anticipating Father telling me how disappointed he was of me.

Father pressed his back to the stable door and lines on his face eased. "Would you like to go to town?"

I released a deep sigh and blinked. "Town?"

Father narrowed his eyes and tilted his head as if confused. "Aye, the market town, Hampton."

"I thought you wished to travel alone?"

"Soon, but it would bring me joy to take you and Mother out today. Winter is approaching."

I smiled. Rarely did I get to venture out.

"Yes. I'm happy. I would love to go." I tamed my excitement, but I screamed with joy inside.

"Don't fidget. Go get dressed. We've got ground to cover."

"Yes, Father." I pressed a kiss to his cheek.

Father gave me a soft grin as his cheeks turned rosy. I looked over my shoulder to Angel and then skipped all the way to the house. The smell of freshly baked bread stopped me from entering my chamber.

"Hungry?" Mother wore her best dress of light-blue wool, and she had pinned her sunrise-gold hair back in braids.

She looked so lovely. Rarely had I seen her dressed in her finest.

"Yes, I'm famished. I could eat a cow." I sat in front of my plate. "You look beautiful, Mother. The dress complements your eyes."

"Thank you." Mother poured me some milk. Her lips pinched in the center and her sky-blue eyes sparkled, as if she was hiding a secret. "I made something for you."

"What is it?" I got out of my seat. I was never the patient one.

Mother tapped my shoulder. "Nay, Jaclyn. After you finish your meal."

Chapter Seven
The Market

Draping the lavender dress in front of me, I used a small hand mirror to see my reflection. The simple dress had long sleeves, but Mother had hand-sewn lace around the cuffs and the bosom. She had also hand-sewed lace at the collar where the dress buttoned up—an elegant garment, fit for a princess.

"It's beautiful, but I don't think—"

Mother frowned and cut me off, already knowing I would give her a mouthful of my contempt.

"We're going to town. People have not seen you for years past. You never know who you'll meet."

Why does it sound like she has some idea who I'll meet?

Mother knew better. I tried to be an obedient daughter, but finding a suitor held no interest for me. I inhaled a deep breath and, instead of my usual pants and tunic, donned the dress Mother had spent many hours sewing.

"Thank you for my lovely dress." I tried to sound cheerful, but words failed me.

Regardless of my stoic tone, Mother's eyes beamed.

"You look so fair and modest. It pleases me to see you clothe yourself like a girl." Mother smiled proudly, clapping her hands together. "Father is preparing the wagon. I've gathered apples, bread, and water. The wagon awaits."

"I'll be right out," I said.

I hoped Mother would give me peace.

With a nod, Mother walked out of my chamber. I opened my dresser and took out the only silver coin I had and shoved it securely inside my boot. Father had gifted it to me a year past, but I had never wanted anything, so I'd saved it.

I had all I needed, and nothing ever caught my eye when we went to market. I intended to buy something for my parents to show them my appreciation. It would be enough to buy a hat for Father and a trinket for Mother.

"Jaclyn." Father's booming voice vibrated through the wall. "We'll leave without you."

I ran out the door with my blue wool cape swaying from side to side behind me. Angel and Daniel were hitched to the wagon, and my parents waited on the seat in front. I jumped in the back with a couple of sheep, a neatly wrapped blanket, and other items Mother had prepared for trade. Father whistled, and the sound of trotting horses filled the air.

Dust clouded around the wagon. I swatted and coughed as it floated near me. The sun faintly peeked through the dome of sugar-white clouds, but it did not give us warmth. In the distance, large pillows of steel-gray clouds drifted our way, and I prayed the rain would not come while we traveled.

Our journey would be long and tiresome, and rain would make it unbearable. Leaning my back against the wagon, I admired the sky and begged, *please don't rain.*

To pass the time traveling, I made up stories along the way. The rolling hills became the castle walls while the sentinel trees guarded us from the monsters living beyond. And I, the princess warrior, kept everyone safe with my sword. But I kept these stories to myself today.

The vast green fields turned brown the farther we traveled. Even the trees lining the road had lost their summer color. They stood naked and barren, the stripped leaves crinkled and lifeless on the ground. The bare branches reminded me of death, but it would all be reborn in the spring.

We snaked along narrow streams, tapered paths, and jolting, rocky roads. The roads reminded me why I didn't like to travel.

The wind whipped into a frenzy. I pulled the hood of the cape over my head to keep the cold from stinging my face. When that did not work, I lay down, tucked my knees to my chest, and drew the cape over me like a blanket.

Cuddling closer to the sheep offered some relief. Eventually, the humming of the wind-song beguiled me, and the wagon rocked me to sleep.

I fluttered my eyes open, still feeling the motion of the wagon. When I peered off to the side, the hills no longer came to view, and serrated, sky-piercing mountains loomed in the distance. White dusted the peaks of the tallest ones. I rejoiced for we had arrived at last.

Father glanced over his shoulder to me. "You had a restful sleep."

"Aye, I did."

"Are you hungry? Would you like bread or water?" Mother

handed me the jug of water.

"Thank you."

After taking a few long gulps, I passed it back to her. Too eager to get moving, I passed on the bread Mother offered.

When Father stopped the wagon, he jumped out and tied Daniel and Angel. Then he helped Mother out. Careful not to dirty my dress, I welcomed Father's help.

Father lifted the neatly wrapped fabric out of the wagon and handed the parcel to Mother. While Mother headed to trade the coverlets she made, I meandered between the homes and shops that seemed too close together after so long in the open hills. They cut the wind, but in turn, half of the road had little sun.

I dropped my hood to bathe in the golden sun and breathe in the cool air as I walked on the pebbled ground. Some people stopped to trade inside the shops while others bargained by the wagons. When I reached the wagon with baked breads, Father took me to the side.

"Here." Father placed a silver coin in my hand.

I blinked in surprise. "For me?"

"For you. For your hard labor."

"But it's too much." I shook my head.

Father folded my fingers into a fist. "It's yours. Go spend it. You're not a child anymore. I trust you will use your good judgment."

I yielded, knowing Father's words were final.

"Oh Father, thank you." I said.

"If something catches your fancy, buy it. Mother and I will be here about." He pointed at a few shops. "Don't go past the butcher.

You remember the butcher's shop?"

"Aye."

I had two silver coins. Two silver coins were better than one, and plenty for me.

I shoved the coin Father had given me inside my boot with my other coin and skipped along. Children's voices and laughter filled the air and the market came to life. A group of children crowded around me, all trying to lure me to their family wagons.

A boy with dirt smeared on his face held up sheep's wool. "For the cold nights."

"Nay." I turned and ran into a girl about the age of ten.

"Pretty fabric for a lovely girl." She shoved it in my face. "Woolen cloth, silk, linens?"

"Nay." I sped up, avoiding the entourage of merchants.

"Cheese to trade," one yelled.

"Sheep, goats, and chickens," another shouted.

The gallimaufry of people and carts, horses, sheep, geese, dogs, and noises filled my head, which was accustomed to the gentle stillness of the hills. The women gossiped while men drank ale, and children ran about with impish grins.

The crowds grew as I walked farther in and amid the tightly packed rows of shops and cottages. My eyes shifted to mackerel, herring, cod, eel, and many more fish glistening in the hay-filled crates inside the carts.

Then I wandered into an area selling sacks of wheat, barley, oats, and rye. Disinterested, I moved along. When I spotted pears, my mouth began to water. It had been a while since I had one.

Weaving around people, I shoved through bodies to look at the merchandise in show windows or handcarts. People stood shoulder to shoulder, bargaining. At last I arrived at the hatter and went inside.

The owner turned my way when the door slammed shut. I glanced at the wall to wall shelves that held hats of various colors and sizes.

"How can I be of service?" He raised his eyebrows when he looked up from his work.

Perhaps he had never seen someone young shopping alone. Maybe he thought I had no money and meant to steal from him. Towering over me, he squinted like I would cause trouble. His sour expression made me feel small as a weasel.

I stood taller and lifted my chin. "I want to buy a hat, sir. I possess a silver coin."

He frowned and examined me like a master to a horse. "You can't buy much with one silver coin, little girl."

Little girl?

"I'm not little." I stomped my foot as heat flushed to my face. "I can buy a hat with a silver coin. Your assistants told me before."

I almost clasped my mouth with my hand, surprised by my rude tone.

He looked behind him to two finely dressed maidens. In the finest silks and wearing pretty jewels around their necks, the ladies turned nosy eyes to me.

He leaned closer. I thought he would scold me. Instead, his tone became softer, and he gave me a fake smile.

"All of our hats are of the highest quality. My boy told false; however, I will hold true to his word. We want no accusation here."

He spoke the last sentence louder, making sure the ladies heard.

Stupid man.

He'd insulted me to make himself appear honest.

He pointed to the bottom wooden shelf lined with simple hats. "Take a peep. Do tell me if one suits your fancy."

My manners strayed. I glared at him and picked up the hat that piqued my interest. Dark brown and made of wool, it looked almost identical to the one Father had. Then I eyed the hats in the middle shelf, but they looked too fancy, so I decided to buy the one I held.

"I want this one, sir."

I handed him the silver coin I'd retrieved from my boot when I'd bent to grab the hat. He had just finished with a lady customer, who paid three silver coins for a fancy red hat with feathers displayed on the top of the shelf.

"One silver as promised." He looked at the ladies, who simpered back at him.

Swindler.

I wished to scrub away his smirk with my boot. He had no idea Father had trained me well. I imagined swiping my feet across the floor in one swift motion and knocking him down. I had done it to Father, and Father appeared stronger than that hare brain.

I dropped the coin in his hand. "Thank you, sir."

I spoke politely, even though I wanted to shove Angel's poop on his head. He said nothing and attended to the next customer while I snickered under my breath, imagining his face covered with dung.

The wind buffeted me when I stepped out, pushing me several

steps forward to jostle a stranger. I apologized, hugged my cape closer, and carried on.

I browsed about the wagons for a trinket for Mother. When nothing held my interest, I treaded toward a wagon that traded brushes and mirrors, but stopped when I saw the meat market and the delicious smell of cooked beef churned my stomach.

I dismissed Father's warning and strayed past the first butcher shop. For Mother, it would be worth the scolding. As I rubbed the coin between my fingers, itching to buy something for her, I pushed the guilt away.

"Just a silver coin for a brush and mirror, handcrafted for the lovelies," the old woman said when I approached her.

She wore a black cape, and a hood covered half her face. Silver hair peeked out around the edges. Long, deep scars began at her mouth and disappeared under the shadow of the hood. The lines, almost like a bear had clawed her cheek, merged with the web of wrinkles around her mouth, puckering the skin like aged apples.

A carved rose accented both the wooden handle of the brush and the back of the mirror. Other sets had flowers such as irises and daisies carved into them. The one that caught my eye had been accented with a leafy vine, climbing like a beanstalk. It looked similar to the brush Mother always used for my hair, but bigger and more elaborate.

I reached out, and just before I touched the brush, the old woman grabbed my wrist. Her probing fingers seemed to be seeking something. I gasped and jerked away from her sharp nails and the coldness of her touch.

"I apologize." I tugged at my sleeve, even though it was already down, for fear she had seen my birthmark.

Her hood shifted and her dark, snapping eyes assured me she had. But when she peered up at me with a small smile, she eased my mind.

"Have a care, please."

Her raspy voice stunned me, as she continued to stare, examining me like I was some kind of novelty.

"I'm sorry," I apologized again. "I want to buy the set for my mother. I have a silver coin."

I showed it to her. Perhaps she thought me a thief like the hat seller.

"Which one suits your fancy?"

She reached underneath her cloak for something—*a dagger maybe?*

My pulse raced. My mind became unsteady. Defeating an old woman would be easy, unless she was a witch. I had heard tales of witches in my younger days, but I'd never paid attention. I wished I had.

I pointed. "That one, please."

She handed me the brush first and then the mirror. I ran my finger across the vine from the bottom, feeling the curves and indentations and the fine texture of the smooth wood. Admiring its beauty, I knew Mother would be pleased.

The old woman's eyes stayed on my covered wrists. No fear showed through them, only recognition or something else unexplainable. Before she could ask me a question, I placed the silver coin in front of her and turned to leave.

"Stop," she said.

I gulped fear down my throat.

Have I done something wrong? What will she ask of me?

All my life, no one had asked me about my birthmarks. I hid them well.

"Yes?" I turned to her, smiling.

"Here, I have a gift for you."

I was foolish enough to think she would give me a silver back, so I opened my hand to her. She dropped three beans in it and closed my fist. When her hand touched mine, she gasped sharply, and her eyes rolled back.

I shuddered at her expression. I wanted to run far from her, but I remained calm when no trickery played from her. But why beans? Not a bag of beans, but three shriveled, gray, speckled beans.

"Nay, thank you."

I tried to open my hand to return them to her, but she held steady onto me. The old fool giving me beans—she must be mad. And I needed to head back to Father.

"You look like your mother. Have 'em." Her eyes bored into mine, and then finally let go. "You'd be wise to hold these fast. A time will come when you are in need. Use them wisely."

I glued my eyes to her mouth as she spoke. Her lips seemed to move too slow. The air around me shifted, and her body spun. *Impossible.* Sucking in a deep breath, I blinked to see clearly again, and ran. I did not even thank her.

What happened? Was she a witch? Or worse, the devil himself?

What did she mean, I looked like my mother? People said I looked like my father. We shared the same brown eyes and dark hair. Mother had blue eyes and golden hair. Mother knew no

55

witches.

Lies. That woman told lies.

After I passed the first meat shop, I turned back to the old woman once more. Though the wagon remained, no sign of her existed. I checked again and again, and even counted to ten, thinking she would appear. Either my mind played tricks on me or she had packed and left.

So quickly?

I rubbed my temples. Perhaps I had seen a witch, or I had been deprived of sleep, but her gift proved she'd existed. Opening my hand, I stared down at the ugliest beans I'd ever seen. What use did I have of them?

"A time will come when you are in need," she'd said.

In need of beans?

I scoffed but did not loosen my fist. Crazy things had been happening. I'd thought about tossing them away or giving them to one of the children passing by, but my gut told me to keep them, so I shoved them inside my boot. Hiding the hat, brush, and mirror under my cape, I dashed to meet my parents.

The night air nipped my nose and my toes. I ate supper in the wagon as we rolled home.

I hid the items I had bought under the bed when I got home. I did not have much space in my room, and Father might find them if I hid them somewhere in the barn.

After I changed into a chemise, I went directly to the fire Father had started. As always, Mother warmed some milk before bed.

Father reminded us he would leave before dawn. Mother packed bread, dried meat, and a jug filled with water for him, while Father readied his other supplies for travel. We said our goodbyes, and I went off to bed thinking about the old woman, unable to erase her from my mind, and the beans still inside my boot.

You look like your mother.

Her words haunted my dreams.

Chapter Eight
The Secret Meeting

father had asked me to tend to the chores while he was away, which I would have done anyway, but I did not plan to be there. Instead I decided late that night to go with him. I wanted to see the beasts they talked about.

Yes, I was scared out of my mind of these monsters, but curiosity gave me reason to be brave. And my haunting dreams nagged me to find out if the monsters and I were connected.

I'd had a vision of them when I'd touched the lance. There had to be a reason. I had to find out. Or I was a stupid fool.

I packed bread, dried meat, and my own jug, and then I snuck inside the wagon and buried myself under a wool blanket already in the back corner.

Three sheep bedded down by the wagon, tied snugly to the wheel kept me company. The poor sheep. He would use them as bait to lure the monsters out. I felt sorry for them. Unable to rub the sleep away, I drifted to slumber.

The movement of the wagon as Father loaded up the sheep startled me awake. Darkness still blanketed the sky. Mother would wake soon and find no eggs or fresh milk. Worse yet, I would be nowhere to be seen. I would receive many days of harsh scolding for my trick, but it would be worth the punishment to see monsters firsthand.

Later, I opened my eyes to the brightness of day, but the sun remained hidden behind the thick, gravel-gray clouds. The bitter air stung my skin from the sudden cold slap from the air. Needing warmth, I blew hot breath onto my fingers. Then I gathered the bits of hay that had spread during the previous day's travel to cover myself more thoroughly, just in case Father decided to check the wagon again.

When my stomach stirred in hunger, I sparingly ate bread and dried meat. Curious as to what my father was doing, I peeked through the slats of the wagon. He was eating, too. I smiled. We rode together, and he wasn't alone.

Without a sword, I'd be no help if bandits threatened him, but I'd brought a dagger with me, one I'd taken from Father's secret place. I prayed I would not have to use it.

I breathed a sigh of relief, thankful when Father stopped the wagon. My full bladder had begun to make the ride unpleasant. When Father got out, he went to a nearby tree. Unfortunately, I did not have that luxury.

Cautiously, trying not to make too much noise, I climbed out, glanced around to make sure no one saw me, and relieved myself next to the wagon. After climbing back inside, I tucked myself in the same position just in time as Father came back, and we rode again.

We passed through the market town we'd visited the day before. People filled the streets and business ran as usual with trading and bargaining. I did not realize how big the town was until we traveled through it.

Usually, we only journeyed to the market and then set out for home to make it before dark. Sometimes the countryside roads were not safe, so the earlier we left, the better.

As we exited the town, the road split in two. When the wagon veered to the left, the landscape changed. The trees thinned as we passed the barren, autumn fields, and the hills gave way to dry, flat plains. We traveled on a dirt road, showing no signs of civilization, and I shuddered in apprehension, for we were on our way to Black Mountain.

The night suddenly became eerie. Branches snapping under the wagon's weight made me jump in the quiet, and my pulse raced at the thought of monsters leaping from behind the trees.

All was fair so far. Father hadn't found out I'd hitched a ride, and I'd acclimated to the harsh cold. But just as those thoughts entered my head, several drops of water fell on my cheek.

Drip. Drip. Drip.

I peered up, half expecting to see a sheep's behind, but more butter-soft drops brushed my face, and the sheep all lay quiet.

Menacing clouds covered the sky, moving faster and darkening every second. Their bellies hovered taut and dangerous, ready to unleash a storm. I flinched as the lightning struck and thunder cracked.

Covering my ears, I shivered under the blanket. Rain began to fall rapidly, then faster, and then came pelting down, like God's strong hands slapping the ground. Within seconds, I was completely drenched.

I quickly ate my last bread before the rain soaked it, but I savored the water, careful not to drink too much. The rain continued until I was a frigid lump, and by the time Father slowed the wagon, darkness cloaked everything outside the glow around the lantern he had next to him, further limiting my view.

Father parked the wagon by a tree, jumped out, and led the sheep down to the ground. Holding my breath, I lay still while he moved. Then other horses and wagons pulled up beside ours, and I stayed low until I thought it safe to peek.

Though plenty, the tall, barren trees gave no shelter from the rain. My teeth chattered and I trembled without cease. My bones and muscles ached and refused to move, not from the long ride, but from the icy wetness. Holding on to the side of the wagon, I pulled myself to my knees and glanced over the side.

I kept my eyes locked on five flickering lanterns.

Only five? Where are the other seven? Cowards.

I spotted Father tugging on the sheep, a sword in his other hand. He'd come ready for whatever he might meet, as had I. I tightened my grip on the dagger as the men trudged up the muddy road, moving farther and farther away from the wagons.

They stopped deeper into the forest. Stray gleams from the lanterns let me know where they stood. Though trees and rain spoiled my view, I spotted Father by the pale sheep next to him. I was certain I would catch a cold, or worse, a fever.

After Father tied the sheep to a tree, the men retreated and hid by another. They had no shelter from the rain under the bare branches, and certainly none from the monsters. I did not know how much time had passed, but even seconds seemed too long, especially when my whole body felt like ice.

"What if the monsters don't come?" The speaker shouted over

the pounding rain and the savage wind.

It sounded like Aldwin. He always had plenty to say.

"If you wish to go home, go. You serve no one," Father replied with a hint of annoyance.

"Perhaps the rain is the problem. The weather is not in our favor, but I doubt if it favors the monsters either." I recognized William's voice.

"Then I'll sleep tonight and wait tomorrow. I've come this far. I will not waste the effort." Father spoke like a true leader. "I'm not going to force you to stay."

"How long will you wait?" asked a voice I did not recognize.

"As long as we must." John's voice? "Stop bickering and be a man. We've just begun."

I moved to the other side of the wagon to get better shelter under the tree, but my vision became severely limited, worse than before. When streaky lightning emblazoned the sky, the horses, including Daniel, stamped and whinnied, but the rope around the tree kept them secure.

In that one-second flash, I saw a silhouette of Black Mountain, and a dark despair seized hold of me all the way down to my marrow. Then, from nowhere, loud shrieks pierced my ears—the same sound I'd heard in my nightmares so many nights.

Pain washed over me, like nothing I'd felt before. I dropped to the wagon on bended knees, struggling to keep the sounds at bay. Soft moans escaped me, but I screamed inside, praying for the pain to stop.

What is happening to me?

But I knew. It came and went without any warning, but it had never happened during my waking hours. The devil had possessed me. I was sure of it.

My body burned, my muscles twitched, my head throbbed, and my fingers and toes felt like pins had pierced every single nail. The need to pull out my hair and pummel my head against the wagon seized me, but I held my limbs tightly. It would soon be over.

I wanted to scream, claw through my skull or stab the dagger into my heart to stop the torture. No release came from the waking nightmare. Then, fast as it had come, it stopped. Relief flooded over me, and I raised my face to the rain. I sighed as the icy water soothed my burning skin, until the sheep began to bleat and struggle against their ties.

I sat up, this time not caring if men saw me. My teeth chattered, and the rain kept falling, and my vision stayed unclear except for the bobbing lights of the lanterns. I could no longer tell where Father stood as I peered into the night, until the sheep bleated louder.

The roar of the monsters whirled in the air—one deafening snarl after the other—and loud thumps steadily approaching shook the earth.

Boom! Boom! Boom!

From the sound of them, there were at least three. Maybe more.

Their rage rumbled the earth like a lion's growl, but a hundred times worse. I wanted to see what they looked like, but the rain and the darkness made it impossible. I had to wipe water off my face every second to better my vision.

When the lanterns moved closer to the sheep, I stiffened. And not too far from them shone six glowing circles—radiant like the sun—high above the ground. My gut told me they were the monsters' eyes, burning like Hell's fire.

God help us.

"What are you waiting for?" Aldwin shouted. "Kill the beasts."

"No, Aldwin," Father said.

"We can't fight giants, Richard."

"May God have mercy."

The angered monsters' cries reverberated within the forest, loud enough to be heard for miles. When lightning struck again, shock slammed into me and my breath hitched, for I got a glimpse of the monsters towering over the men.

Their elongated arms possessed claws the size and shape of swords. To my horror, the beasts looked like the creatures in my vision when I'd touched the lance.

They are real ... real ... real. Taller than life. Claws like a beast. Teeth as sharp as knives. Phantom demons incarnate.

"Run," William shouted, and then human screams followed.

My vision cleared as the rain eased. Looking from left to right, I tried to follow the movement of bodies through the dark. A man flew across the space and collided with a tree. Other men ran, but there was no escape as trees crashed to the ground under the monsters' blows.

Father's men were only supposed to observe. What had gone wrong? Panic seized my heart when I saw only four lanterns.

"The devil killed Aldwin," John yelled.

"Retreat," Father hollered. "Peter, keep safe."

More human shrieks echoed in the night, and only three

lanterns were left, along with two sets of glowing amber lights. What had become of the other pair of eyes?

"It's got William," John groaned.

"Run, John," Father bellowed.

Roars terrorized me.

One lantern swung alone.

"Richard!" John screeched.

Monstrous footsteps shook the ground, fading as they moved away.

Then everything went still.

No sound came but the soft patter of rain. But to me, it was the sound of death. My heart hammered, and all my blood drained to my feet. Paralyzing fear for my father and his fellow men enveloped me, and I bit my bottom lip as I wrapped my fingers around my dagger.

"Father." A whimper rose from my throat.

Shaking and weak at the knees, I forced myself to climb out of the wagon and take cautious steps, holding my dagger in front of me. The squelch of my boots on the muddy ground sounded so loud in the quiet night. The tilted lantern one of the men had dropped gave off a glimmer of light, guiding me, and the rain dying off to a soft wind gave me a better view.

Picking up the blood-spattered lantern in my trembling hand, I tried to calm my breathing as I searched for any sound of life. I even looked for the sheep, but only ropes stained with blood remained tied to the tree.

"Father," I called louder, my voice shaky, and my knees unsteady.

Father did not answer.

My boot hit something sticky. I placed the lantern closer to the ground and gasped aloud to see pools of red liquid. When I raised the lantern a little bit higher, I saw I was surrounded by puddles of crimson.

So much blood … I had never seen so much blood.

Then the light revealed Aldwin's mauled body. His guts had spilled out, and his legs had been ripped off.

Grace of God. Such horror.

My stomach coiled and I fought the urge to vomit. I stumbled back, and the light revealed another body with no head. Moving away from the gruesome sight, I searched for the others, but found no one.

But so much blood … so much blood … everywhere I stepped. How was it possible if only two men had been slaughtered?

Where was Father? My imagination drove me mad, showing me Father's body torn apart.

Oh, please, do not let this be.

When I could not find Father, I felt a bit of relief that he might still be alive. Good news. But then, what had happened to my father, William, and John?

I lifted the lantern higher to get a better view. Larger-than-life footprints marked the ground and the trees were knocked down along the monsters' path. The lantern's light picked out three long ruts gouged in the muddied road and I could no longer see the direction they'd taken in the deep darkness.

I imagined their bodies being dragged all the way to Black Mountain and then carried into Hell.

Chapter Nine
Brave Mother

I ran.

Father and his friends had been taken. Clambering into the front of the wagon with the lantern, I picked up the reins and whistled for Daniel to get moving, but he would not budge.

He knew. He'd heard the beasts. He smelled the blood. He knew Father was not in the wagon with me.

"Daniel, you mustn't be afraid," I beseeched him. "Father is gone. I will not forsake him. I swear we'll get him back, but I must get help."

Speaking the words brought me to my senses. Shock had so numbed me, and the truth hadn't had time to fully register. When reality finally settled in the dark with only Daniel, I felt alone, terrified. Terror and rage had anchored me frozen in a vise-like grip.

Father is gone. What if the monsters came back?

"Daniel. Go." I reached over and gave him a shove on the rear, and he started moving slowly. I understood his hesitation.

He was just as frightened.

Gut-wrenching pain racked me the farther I moved from the horror. I felt in leaving Father, I had assured his death. Tears burned my eyes, and fear for my father ate a hole in my heart. I wept so hard the road blurred until I ran out of tears.

Darkness still covered the sky, but Daniel knew the way home. It would be easier now. Though the rain had stopped, my wet clothes stole my warmth. I did not care.

After hours, I passed the town called Hampton, and I fought to keep my eyes open while I slumped like a beaten rag. Light came from behind the clouds, bringing warmth to the land, and from the position of the sun, I knew it was late afternoon.

Though the bitter wind chilled me, the heat felt good on my face. The fabric of my clothes stuck to my skin and some parts had dried stiff, but they did not bother me. I had no right to complain. Monsters had taken Father.

He had to be alive. I would not rest until he was found.

I did not know how much time had passed, but I had collapsed to the side on the wagon seat. Exhausted and weak, I had passed out like a drunk. When I heard Mother's faint voice, I thought I'd lost my senses, but when it came again I blinked my eyes open.

"Jaclyn," she called again. "For the love of God … ah, lass."

Daniel had brought me home.

Good boy, Daniel.

All kinds of emotions burst in the pit of my stomach. Tears distorted my vision until I wiped them away. Mother in white, like an angel, ran toward me. I shook the reins to urge Daniel to go faster. It did not take long to reach Mother.

"Jaclyn," she said, out of breath. Covering her mouth with her hands, liquid pooled her eyes.

"Mother," I cried out and dropped, almost collapsing on the

ground.

I felt like I'd run all day. I hadn't eaten, and my dry throat scratched like I had swallowed sand. How was I to tell her about Father? I got as far as parting my lips when Mother embraced me tightly enough to crush me, and then battered me with questions.

"Jaclyn, my heart has been in despair. I've been mad with worry. What will your father say?" She stopped and froze. Her eyes fell on Daniel, and then the wagon. "Where is your father?" she asked hesitantly. "Why the tears?" Shivering, she clasped her hands together.

"Pray, be not angry with me, Mother. The monsters—" My lips trembled, and I pointed a shaking hand behind me, as if I could see all the way to Black Mountain. "I hid in the wagon last night and traveled with Father. He did not know. He protects townspeople," I rambled, unsure if I made sense. "They sought monsters from Black Mountain." Tears fell from my cheeks. I gasped for air. The image of ripped-apart bodies flashed through my mind. "The monsters killed Father's friends and they took Father, William, and John."

Mother wiped my tears with trembling hands. As she dried them, her own flowed. "Jaclyn … monsters? Black Mountain?" Her fear was palpable.

I shook my head feverishly, wishing she could see what I'd seen. My gasping and choking on tears made it harder to explain. Mother wrapped her arm around me and patted Daniel's head with the other hand.

Mother wove her fingers through my hair, caressed my face and my arms, as if she needed to know I was well. "Let us go inside and get you out of these clothes. You'll catch fever." Then she unhitched Daniel, guided him to the house, and tied him close to the door. "Bless you for bringing Jaclyn home."

Warmth from the fire engulfed me and my tears subsided. The aroma of something delicious sent a jolt of hunger pangs to my stomach. But eating a meal did not seem fair when Father was in the hands of the monsters.

Mother went to my chamber and returned. She peeled off my clothes and helped me into the fresh ones. Then she handed me some hot cider. One sip spread heat through my body, easing my muscles.

Mother paced back and forth, seemingly deep in thought. After a while, she stopped and sat beside me.

"Tell me everything." She looked at me sternly, her eyes demanding the truth. "Don't leave anything to the imagination."

So I did. She listened with no hysterics or crying. Mother proved to be a strong woman.

"I need to go to town. I must find William's sons. Their family needs to be told. I shall gather men and travel to Black Mountain." She stood up. "First, let me feed you. You must be starving."

She brought me a bowl of soup and bread. I wanted to swallow it all in one gulp, but I remembered my manners. Then I dipped the bread into the soup and took a bite. Oh, it tasted heavenly.

"While you eat, I'll put the wagon back inside the barn and give Daniel a bucket of grain and brush him down. I'll need to ride him to William's town if he can make it. If you can recall, he has three sons. Jack is the youngest. You remember him?"

"Aye."

Jack's older brothers were muscular and tall, over six feet, while Jack had been scrawny and short, but scandalously bold with the girls. It had been at least a couple of years since I'd seen him last, but who was counting? Still, I would have rather kissed a pig than associate with him.

"I shall come along, Mother." I took another mouthful of soup.

Mother placed her hand on my shoulder to stop me. "Nay. You need to rest and warm up. You've traveled far in this wretched condition. You'll catch fever or worse."

I looked down at my shaky hand holding the bowl. Drops of the soup fell to the floor. I agreed, but only because I had a plan of my own.

Mother went to her chamber, then returned wearing a man's tunic and breeches, and with her hair tied back. With more layers of clothing and a cape around her, she looked warmer and less feminine.

Women should not ride alone, especially at night. When the sun dipped lower, the ride would be dangerous. Hopefully it would be a lonely road, and no one would be around.

After she grabbed a water skin and stashed bread inside a cloth, she gave me a kiss on the forehead.

I reached out my hand to hers. "Are you certain? Father would not approve."

"Father is not here and he needs me. I may be a woman, but women have their own bravery. Stay by the fire. I fear to leave you alone. Father left his sword under the bed. I'll be back by tomorrow's sunset."

When she opened the door, the brisk wind almost blew out the fire. Mother had to bend low, fighting to pull the door shut. So brave. Courageous. I had never seen Mother with such resolve and fire in her heart. And I must follow her example.

Father had left his sword behind?

I recalled his special sword. He must have taken that one.

I tossed a couple of pieces of wood into the fire and listened for the sound of Mother leaving. When I finished the last of my soup and bread, I went to my chamber to change into dark, wool breeches and a thick, long-sleeved tunic. Then I put on my cape and headed for the barn.

Chapter Ten
The Black Mountain

ne decision can change the course of fate.

What if I hadn't eavesdropped on Father at the barn? What if I hadn't followed Father? Perhaps it would have taken the two days he'd said he would be gone, plus more, to figure out he had been missing.

Maybe I would have never found out at all, if the men who remained told no one of their true mission. No one would dare travel to that road to seek answers.

People would have assumed bandits had killed Father and his friends. Then I remembered the bloody bodies. Bless their souls for standing by my father and for their courage.

Mother had told me to stay safe and keep warm, but I didn't listen. Father needed me. Every precious second wasted determined his fate. I did not plan on waiting for a search party.

I imagined their conversation. They would agree how dangerous it would be. They might argue about how to get to Black Mountain. It might take days for them to organize or make the decision to go.

Father did not have time. I had to go forth. I had to be brave.

I opened the secret hoard. Father's sword was gone. *So he did take it.* I had already taken out the dagger I'd left in the wagon, so

I retrieved the second dagger and placed it inside my boot.

Would two daggers be enough?

I'd thought about taking Father's second sword, but Mother needed something with which to defend herself. The only thing left was the lance—too long to carry—and I liked it not.

Twice I had seen a vision when I'd touched the sharp point. Did I dare do it again?

Once more, curiosity held me strong. I had to know if another vision would appear. Instead of picking up the lance, I reached down to touch the sharp point—an image of a man sprang into my mind.

I jumped back and gasped, not because I was scared, but because the man stared back at me intensely, as if angry I had seen him. Had he seen me? Ridiculous. But I had seen him. Strangely, he had left me with a feeling of sadness. For reasons unknown, I felt his emotions as if they were mine.

His light brown hair danced with the wind and midnight blue eyes sparkled. With high, defined cheekbones and a strong nose, he looked like any ordinary man, except he had a scar on his left cheek, three inches long and thick. As before, the image lasted briefly, but stayed long enough to imbed in my mind.

One minute, the desire to fight and take on a whole slew of monsters had filled me, and the next, my heart held a somber ache. How odd. Regardless, fighting monsters by myself was stupid. If I were not clever, I would become their dinner.

I closed the compartment and walked to the next stall.

"Good day, Angel." I brushed her mane. "Ready? You must ride faster than the wind. Father needs you, you hear?"

74

After I saddled her, I fetched a water skin and a cloth filled with bread, and found a place to stuff them inside the saddle pockets.

I never looked back, never thought twice about my actions, only moved onward to find Father. Some might proclaim I'd set myself on a suicide quest.

The result did not look hopeful, but remaining at home did not sit well with me. I refused to be afraid. It would only make me slower and weaker.

Bless my Angel. She felt my desperation. She galloped in great strides. When I reached the split in the road, I veered to the left as the sun lowered to follow Father's path.

Every way I turned looked lifeless—not a single soul could be seen or heard. No birds sang, no squirrels scuttled along the tree trunks, and no leaves danced in the breeze.

What was left of the forest appeared dead. Bare branches dropped, and the cracked trunks withered like wrinkles on aged skin. If death had a face, I had seen it.

A haunting unease filled my senses the farther I moved along, causing me to question my sanity. Ghosts without faces and soft cries I knew not to be real possessed my mind. The self-created illusions followed in my wake, and my lungs squeezed as fear took hold of my muscles.

Breathe. Breathe. They are not real. Lies and tricks the ancient forest sends to scare me away.

No matter what I had told myself, the forest appeared to cave in and the sharp-tentacled branches seemed to claw at my flesh. I fought the urge to turn back and run at every step.

Closing my eyes, I cradled closer to Angel and pulled the hood over my head, wanting to disappear into happier days, but the sounds … Oh, the sounds. The haunting whispers pulled me back to their deadly intent. I did my best to shut them out.

When I reached the area where I'd seen the dismembered bodies, I shielded my face, but it did little good. Peering between my fingers, I found bloodstained areas in the dirt, but no corpses. I dropped my hand and swept the grounds with my eyes, but still nothing.

Only one explanation came to mind: wild animals had had their fill.

Angel edged past the bloodstains and trotted farther into the forest. Weird shapes rose around me, covered in leafless, woody vines, but too large and angular to be natural. Houses had once stood there, and the forest had nearly reclaimed them.

I shoved a fist to my mouth, stifling a scream. Sheltered by a mossy stone wall, a gaping skull stared at me from underneath a bramble bush. And a glimpse of pale bones seemed to taunt me from under the choking vines.

After I struggled to pass the heap of fragmented trees, a murky swamp blocked my way, so I rode around its edges. Angel reared and whinnied when she had to step in it, and I shushed her too late. I worried we had attracted attention.

When I reached the base of Black Mountain, I jumped off Angel and tied her to the closest tree, loosely in case she needed to run away from wild animals. I wanted to hide her, but nothing seemed big enough to cover her. I also left the lantern with her so I could spot her easily.

During my journey, I had not doubted I would find Father,

but as I tilted my head to survey what I was to climb—as black as midnight in the fading light—doubt crept in.

Ridges, curves, and outcroppings of rock formed the giant edifice. But about halfway up, it was nothing but smooth, slanted surface, and clouds covered the peak. The mountain showed me no end.

How am I to climb? You can do this.

No time to fret. I would figure it out once I got to that point. I ascended, one foot after the other, until the sun stretched and dipped even lower toward the horizon. I had thought about carrying the lantern with me, but it would have only gotten in the way, and the breeze would have blown out the flame.

Sometimes my cloak caught the wind, dragging me sideways. The frigid air blew relentlessly, challenging me. I clutched tighter, but my numbed fingers made it difficult to hold steady. A few times I almost lost my grip, but I carried on.

I was halfway up the mountain when darkness crept slowly across the land. The silver moon and diamond stars seemed closer and brighter. They were my only companions, so I kept my eyes on them. But the hike was just the beginning. Tilting my head up, I stiffened. My muscles ached, tired.

Must continue to climb for Father. Do not stop now. Keep going.

Every slap from the wind became a battle. Every inch became a struggle, as my lungs filled with the heavy frosty air. My trembling body, like the icicles on the frozen trees, begged me to stop and find warmth, but I carried on.

The monsters would not be the death of me; I would die climbing that treacherous mountain.

I found a place to rest where my footing steadied. Knowing I had to use my daggers since the mountain had become steeper, I took one out from my boot and clenched it between my teeth. Then I took out the other one.

Feeling something bumpy inside my boot, I stuck my finger inside. A pebble must have gotten inside it. When I pulled it out, I saw one of the beans the crazy woman had given me. Then it blew out of my hand.

With the events of the past couple of days, I hadn't thought about them. Even when Mother had helped me change, I'd slipped my feet right back in and had not felt them.

The foolish old woman had said I would need them someday, but that did not mean it was true. Yet I found it strangely sad that I'd lost one.

How in the world can a tiny little bean help me?

I brushed the thought aside. I had no time to dwell. One after the other, I wedged the daggers into the cracks of the sheer mountain face and used them as handholds.

Not so bad. For Father, I must climb. Hurry. I chanted repeatedly for courage and strength.

There were two problems. Finding a solid spot to get my footing seemed almost impossible the farther I climbed, and my limbs continued to shake with cold and exhaustion.

An eerie shiver ran through me. Long gouges marked the face of the mountain, indicating what I already knew. The monsters had sharp claws.

From far away, the mountain did not look half so steep. I had to decide—keep moving with the possibility of dying as my body gave out or go back down.

Tears stung my eyes and I sobbed. So tired. So tired. So tired. My muscles protested.

No. No. No. Please, someone help me.

I should have waited for Mother, but deep down I knew no one would help the captured men. Who would be crazy enough to do so? Fate had made my choice for me.

I pulled out the left dagger to wedge in another crack, but my foot slipped and I lost my balance. Cursing under my breath, I kicked wildly, seeking a foothold.

My stomach dropped. I slammed against the face of the mountain. I slapped the wall to clutch to something, anything.

My chest, arms, and legs scraped against the surface as I plummeted. Poor judgment, stupidity, and stubbornness would kill me. Still holding on to the daggers, at last, I tumbled over a precipice overhanging a ravine and fell freely, screaming.

They say when you face death, you see days long past, but I did not. The image of the man I had seen when I'd touched the lance flashed before me, the face and the scar clearer than before.

The sorrow in his eyes grew heavier, watching me fall. My mind seemed possessed by the demon before my demise. Any second, death would come, and I prayed my soul would find salvation.

I closed my eyes, seeing my mother and father's faces, and silently telling them how much I loved them. And my Angel. Who would take care of her? My mother. What would become of her if her daughter and husband never returned?

The thought of leaving my mother alone in the world crushed

me.

I couldn't die. My life had just begun.

I fell faster and faster as air swooshed around me. I had no choice but to surrender to death.

Then I felt only the ache of slamming into the ground, which made sense, but it did not crush me. I had expected pain beyond what a human could bear. Instead, my stomach settled and my heart beat steadier as I felt myself rise off the ground.

Up and up and up I soared. A different kind of fluttering sensation took over. Butterflies swirled in my stomach frantically as if caged inside.

I shot my eyes open to a blanket of stars, like flashing pinpricks in a wall of darkness, and felt as though I were being carried to them. *Impossible.* Reaching to the right and left of me, I fanned my fingers out over a cool, ridged surface.

When I flipped over, my stomach jumped to my heart and Mother's soup rose to my throat. A giant, fast-growing beanstalk lifted me higher and higher off the ground. Digging my fingers into the leaf's spongy yet firm surface, I held on for dear life.

Is it a dream?

I'd died and a vine was carrying me to Heaven? But my lantern and Angel, so tiny, were where I'd left them, shrinking as I flew.

The bean came to mind. I hadn't suspected powerful magic inside such a small, ugly thing. My head spun with many questions, but I surrendered to wonder.

The old woman had saved my life.

Not witch or devil, but an angel perhaps. Why me?

I stopped thinking and took pleasure in the ride as I punched through endless layers of misty clouds that cloaked everything below me. The vine took me right where I needed to be.

The unforgiving wind calmed to a whisper, but the freezing air remained. No monsters awaited. Just some dried, short hedges by the entrance of the cave, veiled by thick haze, and a flickering torchlight from inside.

I worried the beanstalk would shrink back down to a bean or wither when I stepped off, but it did not. I would not know the way down if the beanstalk disappeared. The other two beans pushed against my skin inside my boot; I would hold them for dear life.

After blessing the beanstalk—foolish thought—and thanking God and the old lady, I felt my confidence blossom.

With only two daggers by my side, I cautiously paced to an entrance of a dark cave ... a devil's home.

Chapter Eleven
Monsters' Cave

ear and I had been best enemies since last night when my father had disappeared, but I'd never experienced it more intensely than I did at that very moment. It coiled around my heart.

A breeze caressed against me like a ghost's touch, and musty air infused my nose. I welcomed it after the stinging wind outside.

No sounds of monsters greeted me.

My hand trembling, I held out my daggers, ready to strike as my boots scraped with every cautious step. I would not have thought monsters would make time to put up torchlights, yet torches hung every few feet.

Chills prickled down my spine. I gasped and halted when giant footprints, not just two or ten, but countless stamped the dirt. By the size of the footprints, my estimation of their height was not far off. The ceiling reached high, about thirty feet.

Oh God. What have I done?

How was I to survive? One of me and at least hundreds of them. I had willingly offered myself to be the monsters' dinner—a mouse inside a lion's den with no way out.

No. Stop thinking, Jaclyn. You mustn't think. Father needs you. You have no choice. In your heart, you know no help will come. Have faith.

I willed my courage and crawled ahead, aware of every sound.

Gouges marked the cave wall on either side of me the farther I walked in. As I examined and followed the marks, a haunting ancient tune whispered in my ear, coaxing me by turns to leave or stay. But I did not fear it. I knew the soft hums were not from the beasts.

Then I caught the sound of a gentle flow of water, which gave me some comfort, but I knew better than to ease my guard. Monsters lived in the cave. No peace awaited me.

Gripping my daggers tighter, I waited for monsters to jump at me. Only my shadow followed, changing its position as I walked.

Footsteps echoed behind me. I looked over my shoulder every few feet, but there was no one there except a family of rats scurrying away. I breathed a sigh of relief, but it died quickly, when the cave opened to a cavern, split by a ravine.

A new world materialized before me. Countless torches glowed bright as a sunrise. A long, rickety bridge separated me from the other side. Below, the darkness of the abyss stilled my heart. I listened for the monsters, and when I heard nothing, I crept ahead.

The wooden bridge swung when I stepped on it. The gaps between the planks stirred my imagination. I envisioned a hand thrusting through and grabbing my ankle.

I tried not to think about the bridge collapsing, for if it did, nothing would stop my fall into the endless, dark pit. With my heart pounding and my knees shaking, I trudged ahead. Each step, I prayed, took me closer to Father.

When I reached the end, I shuddered with relief, but no giants appeared. Had I adventured to the wrong mountain? Surely, the long claw markings on the wall, the footprints, and face of the mountain told the true path.

Who would be foolish enough to visit there, let alone live near the monsters? Again, I looked over my shoulder at a rustle behind me, sensing someone watching me. Nothing. When no one appeared, an eerie shiver raised goosebumps on my skin.

I marched ahead softly, my boots grinding into pebbled ground. My eyes roamed to the high ceiling and then the emptiness ahead. I reminded myself the monsters were giants, and I was their meal.

Farther in, lanterns and torches gave off brighter light to my right. I hid behind the closest boulder when I spotted people.

People moved under the torchlight. Their faces pale as ghosts, they dragged their bare feet, leaving behind a trail. Then I saw all were men, bare-chested and only wearing torn breeches. What were they doing there?

I scurried from boulder to boulder, getting closer to observe their actions. Their faces, necks, arms, chests, and all visible flesh were marked with fresh scars, raw but bloodless. Grime and dried blood caked their skin as if they hadn't washed in months.

'Twas the monsters' doing?

I moved closer, careful not to alarm them. A village of men lived there. Far to my left, sheep milled about inside wooden bars. Then I saw more people. More men lay on the hay in slumber near a narrow stream, and many wood fires burned. Some gathered to warm themselves at the flames.

I searched for Father and his friends. Not seeing them, I stayed in the darkness and hid behind the boulders as I pushed on. My chest heaved and sickness crawled in my stomach, but curiosity bedeviled me.

Blood and torn flesh hung from people's faces. I turned away and tried to gaze beyond, but the closer I got, the more difficult it became to look away.

Pushing past the gruesome village, I climbed up a slope and resumed my search deeper into the cavern. I stopped when I saw a man at an old wooden table large enough to seat twelve, eating a feast fit for a king.

The lantern on the table flickered over his bare back and chest. His shoulders were broad, and his chest was as bronzed as his features from the sun's touch. The large muscles on his arms tightened and flexed as he tore the meat with his teeth.

Grime, dried blood, and open wounds covered the shirtless man, just like the other people, as if an animal with long claws had slashed at his chest.

Who is he?

My mouth watered from the overpowering smell of roasted meat, and I wanted to steal his beef. The rumbling in my stomach turned to hunger pain, but it would have to wait. Food had been the last thing on my mind until I'd seen and smelled the feast. I wondered how the other people could ignore it.

Strangely, no one glanced in his direction, as if they would be punished for it. The people also did not speak. No voices echoed in the cave; only the dragging of their feet, the crackling from the wood fire, and the sheep milling about broke the silence.

I slid down a boulder, tucked my knees and the daggers into my chest, and tried to wrap my mind around what I'd seen as I closed my cloak around me for warmth. Nothing made sense. Knowing they could not see me, I took a moment to breathe.

I needed to find Father, but it would have to wait till they were asleep, and I also needed rest. Tired, hungry, and weak, I leaned my head on the rock. Before I closed my eyes, my thoughts drifted to a happy home and the safety of my bedchamber.

Something cold on my face awakened me. I opened my eyes and sat up. Fear replaced the peace and stillness when I recalled where I was. The daggers had fallen from my hands. I picked them up and pulled them close to my chest.

The rays through the cracks in the cave above told me the sun had risen. The light seeped through many tiny holes that had been impossible to see the night before.

Peeking around the boulder that was three times my size, I did not see a soul except for the sheep. Even the man who had been eating had gone, but when I stood, I jumped back in surprise. The people laid on the ground in slumber. All of them.

Cautiously, I stepped out of my safety and tried to edge around them, but it was not possible. They lay side to side, filling up the space. Step by step, I held my breath as my pulse quickened with each stride, my daggers ready.

A closer look confirmed they were all men. They had almost healed completely. Their skin started to glue itself together. The blood, long claw marks, and broken skin—almost gone. By the grace of God … A miracle? Or the work of the devil?

The image of them waking up—or worse, pulling me down—invaded my mind. Those thoughts weakened my courage. With my daggers ready to strike, I moved faster and held my breath until

I arrived on the other side.

I'd made it to the table where the man had sat alone eating. I grabbed a piece of bread, a chunk of cheese, an apple, and took bites of the meat. I wanted to take more, but I did not want the man to start questioning.

As I bit the apple, sweet juice filled my mouth. Needing to quench my thirst and feed my hunger, I moved far back, taking bits of bread and cheese. The icy draft that drifted over my skin made me tremble, as no sunlight penetrated the area.

The trickling of a gentle stream caught my attention, and I halted to watch it snake around the bend into the darkness. Then wooden bars appeared at the corner of my vision as I was about to take another bite. A prison?

A body with a dark cape hunched by the wall, and next to him two more curled on the ground. Father and his friends? Then I saw the hat with a hole. Father's hat. I'd never been so happy to see that hole.

I picked up a handful of stones as the foul smell of urine wrinkled my nose.

"Father?" I whispered. My heart blazed with warmth.

No answer.

"Father?" I threw pebbles at the sleeping body.

Still no answer.

A few rats scurried away, disturbed.

"Father," I said, a bit louder.

Bodies shifted and stretched as if waking from a long sleep.

A man whipped around, rubbing his eyes. "Jaclyn?"

Chapter Twelve
The Prisoners Found

"Father. I found you at last."

My heart burst with happiness, and I wiped the tears pooled in my eyes.

I shook the wooden bars. Yanking at the poles did no good. Desperately, I tugged and pulled. Nothing. Foolish of me to think I had the strength to break the bars. Surely Father and his friends had tried.

Father rushed to me and gripped the wooden poles between us. His brown eyes, darker in the shadows, grew wider, unbelieving. Dirt and mud caked his face, hair, breeches, and cape.

"Jaclyn."

His scolding tone shocked me.

"What in the heavens are you doing here? How ... how did you get here? How did you even know I was here?" His eyes searched mine with fright.

I had never seen his irises so big before, and I had never heard Father curse until then. I shifted to the two men who rose to stand next to him.

"Is this Jaclyn? It's been far too long. She's grown up." William smiled at me, his green eyes glistening in the torchlight.

"It's nice to see you again." I gave him a wry smile with a quick bow.

Then his expression changed. His lips thinned to a line and his eyebrows arched with concern. "I'm most surprised to see you here. I do not know how or why you are here. 'Tis impossible."

"Good day. I'm John. I've never had the pleasure to meet such beauty," a man said. I dropped my head and looked back up. "It's nice to make your acquaintance."

They were both filthy like my father, and they smelled foul. With long faces and bags under their eyelashes, they did not look well. Father's grunt caught my attention.

"Run, Jaclyn. Go home. Where's your mother? She doesn't know you sneaked away, eh? She must be sick with worry." His tone turned somber, and he dipped his head lower.

I shamefully shook my head. I'd disobeyed and lied, but I had no choice. "Mother went to William's town to gather men." I turned to William. "She went to tell your family. Your sons will come for you, and so will men from your town."

"The men are cowards." William's face twisted in disgust. "They will not come. They would not come with us. If they had, perhaps fate would be different."

"I did not see the monsters. Where are they?" I looked over my shoulder.

The people still slept, recovering. I wondered what would happen to them when the healing completed.

"How do you know about the monsters?" Father's shoulders slumped and he clenched the bars tighter. "Who told you?"

"I can explain later. Now is not the time, Father."

"I don't know where the monsters are," John answered,

running his hand through his hair. "The three of us awoke in this prison. We had been captured, dragged, somehow carried up the mountain, and dumped here." He gazed down to a small lock. "You need to find the key, but I'm afraid it's nearly impossible."

"What happened when you were captured?" I asked.

William shook his head and looked off into the distance. "So many things you do not know, and what I'm about to say will not make sense to you. But there are monsters, Jaclyn. The kind of monsters you only dream of in nightmares. We were only supposed to observe, but Aldwin rushed out. He got scared when he saw their size and their deadly amber eyes. He stabbed one with his sword, over and over, as if the devil took hold of him. Blood flowed everywhere. We fought for our lives, and they killed Aldwin and Peter. Then darkness covered our minds like night. And here we are. We cannot fight back. Our swords are missing."

Blood flowed everywhere.

"Jaclyn."

Father captured my attention.

"You must leave."

I did not reply. Instead, I ran to the table, gathered food, and ran back to the cell. Then I shoved food through the spaces between the poles. They thanked me and took it graciously.

As they ate the cheese, bread, and meat, I went back to grab the cup and filled it by the stream. After making sure it was drinkable, I took the cup to my father and his friends. I had to figure out how to get them out, but for the time, I would help satisfy their necessities.

Taking out my dagger, I tried to cut through the wooden pole, but it was too thick. There had to be another way besides needing a key.

"Where did the people come from?" I asked.

They stopped chewing, gazing at me.

"What people?" Father wiped his lips with the back of his hand. He finished the apple down to the core.

"People that live here," I answered hesitantly.

"Why would these people live with the monsters? Did you try to talk to them?" Father asked, eyeing the dagger peeking from my boot.

I froze. Did Father recognize it? If so, he didn't say. I opened my mouth to answer his question, but stopped. How could I explain what I'd seen?

"They're ... I don't think I can talk to them. They don't speak. You must see for yourself."

"Give me the other dagger," Father said.

When I did, he tried to cut a pole. He strained and then began whittling, slicing away bits like you'd peel a fruit. The sturdy pole seemed unbreakable. Then William stopped Father with a hand on his shoulder.

"Listen." William's eyes grew wide with alarm. "Do you hear? Someone is coming."

While they went back to the positions they had been in before, I scurried away into the shadows. I hid behind the curve of the cave, hidden away with my dagger clutched in front of me.

The same man I'd seen earlier, the one who had been eating alone, approached the prison. I caught a glimpse of his brown hair under the torchlight, and when he turned in my direction, I froze.

Even though he could not see me, his thick, long scar showed—the same scar I'd seen when I'd touched the lance and just before I'd fallen off the mountain.

Turning his attention back to the prison, he sniffed again like a wolf smelling prey. Then he angled his body in my direction. I stiffened and held my breath. My heart hammered faster the longer he remained there.

I jumped back when he rattled the wooden pole.

"Rise!"

His voice—hoarse and deep—how I imagined the devil's voice would sound.

Father and his friends held still. Father waited for the man to open the cell, and when he did, Father would use the dagger he had taken from me to make his escape. But the man only shouted, never attempting to go in. Finally, his nose tilted to the ceiling as if catching a scent, and he walked away with a smirk.

When the path cleared, I placed my dagger inside my boot. Then a hand covered my mouth, and another seized my waist. My heart soared with fear. The scarred man captured me?

He moves with demonic speed.

"Shhh. Be still," he whispered, pressing his chest against my back. "I'll not hurt you. I am going to release you, so quiet yourself."

I cursed myself for shoving my dagger inside my boot and for being a stupid fool. Frightened, I nodded to comply, but I did not plan to listen. Despite a small waist and dainty bones, I had loads of strength and wit.

My father's defense training served me well. Tightening my

muscles, I bent my elbow and jabbed him in the ribs. Then I hooked his ankle forward with my foot, causing him to fall back. I assumed he did not see that coming, especially from a girl, and I went for my dagger.

He still gripped my cape tightly, and I fell on top of him. Our bodies parted on impact. When I rolled to my back, he was on top of me. Pinning my arms over my head, he gave me a sweet, roguish smirk I'd seen before, though I could not remember from whom.

My lips parted to scream, but I would have called attention. I tried to kick, but he straddled my legs. He knew what to do, like a trained fighter. When I got a closer view, I realized no scar marked his smooth face. And his beautiful eyes shone like emeralds, glinting in the lamplight.

I eased the urgent tension just a tiny but, but my muscles stayed guarded, ready to pounce.

He mesmerized me with his handsome, genteel face—sparkling green eyes, lovely but manly cheekbones, his strong jaw, and his supple lips. I longed to kiss him when he bestowed a grin upon me, making my senses reel. And I liked the way he looked at me with such admiration, as if he saw beyond my dirty face.

What in the Lord's name is the matter with me?

My head seemed to float, an intense sensation I never felt before burned through me until I realized I had no idea who the man was.

He got up and offered his hand, but I did not take it. Instead I dusted my clothes to slap away the heated feeling from his closeness.

I backed away. With no words to say, I studied him.

He stood over six feet tall, with broad shoulders, a deep chest, and thick arms. His hips were lean, and his breeches hugged strong thighs.

I'd seen the way Father exercised his muscles in the barn by pulling himself up on a rafter. Perhaps this man did the same. But I was not pleased with myself. He inspired unseemly emotion in me. When he studied me boldly, assessing me, something warm sizzled through my veins. He wasn't trying to hide his gaze, and I did not reprimand him when I did the same.

"What do you want?" I asked fiercely, keeping my voice low. "Do you not have better manners than to sneak up on a girl in the dark?"

My will forsook me, and my eyes roamed over his body again. *Stop staring, you dolt. Stop. Stop. Stop.*

"Jaclyn." My name rolled off his tongue as if we had been longtime friends. "I know you like what you see, but we must move."

Rude and arrogant.

I crossed my arms. "I will not. First, who says I liked what I saw? And who are you?"

The man raised his brows, like I should have known. "First, you just admitted you were looking at me. And second, it's been years, Jacky. 'Tis me, Jack."

He raised his arms wide, greeting me warmly and inviting my stare.

I gasped. The Jack I knew was shorter than me, skinnier than a stick, and looked more child than man. From what I recalled, Jack could charm his way into anything. Girls surrounded him,

94

hoping to get his attention, but I found him annoying.

Untrue. He had been my childhood secret crush.

I'd often wondered what had happened to him. I would not be surprised if he were wed with children. Mayhap he had many wives in many towns. That would not surprise me either.

Brushing my hair away from my face, I studied him boldly. Aye, 'twas Jack after so long. No other soul called me Jacky. Then I was no longer sixteen, but the little girl who had a secret crush on him and the one who was always mad at him for some stupid reason.

With my hands on my hips, I stood my ground. I would not allow him to belittle me and call me such stupid names as if we were still children.

I slowly curled my lips at my wicked thought. "I see you finally grew some balls."

My parents would have demanded I wash my mouth with soap if they had heard me say such a word.

He smiled, a mocking curl of the lip, twisting not to laugh as his eyebrows lifted. "I did not know you cared so much about them. I will give you a peek, if you'd like."

My face flushed hotter than the summer sun. I didn't know what he would say, but certainly not that. I would not admit defeat.

"Nay, thank you. I am sure they are smaller than a weasel's."

He laughed.

"Why did you come here?" I crossed my arms.

He took a step closer, his forehead creasing. "Why have *I* come? The question is, why have you? You are a blockhead, aren't you?"

"I'm not a little girl—and do not call me a blockhead." The

words were said through gritted teeth.

I'm not a little girl? Had I just said that? I wanted to smack myself.

"I have eyes. I can see. You are a woman in every way." His brows twitched playfully, and he tilted his head. "Except perhaps in dress."

My fists tightened to punch him in the face, but he was right. Like me, he wore dark pants, a long-sleeved brown tunic, and a black cape. I opened my mouth to say something, but Father called my name in a loud whisper. Because I'd hidden behind a boulder, he couldn't have seen my tussle with Jack. I should have answered, but instead I explained about the capture.

"My father, your father, and John went to lure the monsters from hiding, and now they have been taken by the monsters, and I—"

"Came alone?" His eyes judged me. "You want to die?"

He had no right to look at me with disdain and to scold me like a father would a child.

"Nay, I'm not stupid, Jack. But someone had to come. How did you know to come here?"

"Your mother came to our town. While my brothers gathered men to rescue our father, I left on my own for Black Mountain. I doubted anyone would step forward to help. People can be selfish. People expect help from their neighbors, but when some seek their aid in turn, they have some excuse. They forget all the good others have done for them. I do not wish to be a coward. Lucky for you, our town is closer to the mountain than your house, or you would be alone right now. Besides, I had a feeling something wasn't right when my father didn't come back as promised. I am not one to wait." He took a step back, gawking at me again. "You've grown up, Jacky. You're brave. I give you credit for that. But you shouldn't have come alone."

"But you did."

"I'm stupid too. I had no choice."

I wrung my fingers on my cloak, anger spiking my pulse. "Neither did I."

His words goaded me to anger. Intending to prove my fighting skills, I grabbed his cape. Instead of mockery, warmth and concern filled his eyes. I loosened my grip.

The heat I felt toward him overwhelmed me, and I stepped away hastily. We needed to save the men first.

"Did you grab me because you want a kiss?" He smirked.

I pushed him away, feeling peevish. For heaven's sake, we had no time for pleasant banter. Our fathers waited to be saved, mere feet away.

"You're impossible. I would not kiss you even if my life depended on it."

"Really?" He raised his eyebrows in mock surprise. "Why not? You haven't kissed me yet. It might not be so bad. You can try and see if you like it."

I shook my head and clucked my tongue. "You were following me, weren't you?"

I recalled hearing footsteps. I'd thought I'd lost my mind. He must have climbed up the beanstalk or caught a ride as it grew. The mountain was impossible to climb.

"Someone had to. Besides, you need my help, and I need to

rescue my father, your father, and John. We can do it together."

I pulled out the dagger from my boot and pressed it against his neck in one swift move. "I'm doing well on my own. Get in my way and I won't think twice about stabbing you right through the heart."

My words were a bit fierce, but I meant them. I stepped back and headed to Father.

"Through the heart?" Jack followed me. "So harsh."

I snickered under my breath, hiding my smile. He had far too much pride and did not need to know I found him charming.

Chapter Thirteen
This Man

Father saw me come out of the shadows. He gazed beyond me to Jack as he stood beside me.

"Jack." William sat up. He looked happy and then worried, reaching through the bars to touch Jack's shoulder. He gave a proud smile, but then his expression changed. "Where are the others?"

Jack shook his head. "I came first. The others lagged, and I grew impatient. Men are gathering. I'm sure of that, but you know it takes time."

William frowned and his eyes filled with sorrow. "I know." Looking up with conviction, he said, "Take Jaclyn and go."

John scrambled to his feet. "Have you lost your mind? What are you saying?" He looked at Jack. "Go find the key, boy."

William grabbed John by his cape and slammed him against the poles. "This is *my* boy, not yours. I'm going to forgive you, for you don't have children. You don't understand. He's my flesh and blood, you hear? He's everything to me. I die before he does. I know Richard feels the same."

He shoved John out of the way.

John flattened his back against the wall and kept quiet. Father looked at William and nodded. They had an unspoken understanding.

"Go, Jaclyn. Go with Jack." Father's eyes softened, begging.

I placed my hand over his on the pole as tears threatened to fall. My heart shattered to see Father, a strong man I admired, look overcome and weak. I would never be able to forgive myself if I let him die in a monster's prison. I'd come too far.

I shook my head. "I will not, Father. I shall return."

I quickened my step before Father could protest. When footsteps scraped on the floor behind me, I assumed Jack had followed.

"Where do you think you're going without me?" he asked.

I spun around with my dagger lowered but ready. "Without you? I don't need your permission or help. If you want to help them, fine, but don't get in my way."

He chuckled, but it died in his throat. My heart skipped a beat in the most unpleasant way. I stood like a deer, poised for flight, but I dared not run.

The scarred man stood in a ray of sunlight and glared at me.

His blue eyes, cold as stone, pinned me still. His shoulders tightened, his fists rounded, and his lips pressed in a grim line. The open wounds on his face and chest had healed as if never there, but the scar remained. He looked like an ordinary man, but I knew he was not.

Jack yanked me behind him. I understood he wanted to be chivalrous, but this only made me angrier.

"Going somewhere?" The scarred man's voice was calm but deadly.

Cold slithered through my veins, as if a venomous snake had

bitten me.

Jack took his dagger from his belt and held it in front of him. "Who are you? Where are the monsters?"

The scarred man's eyebrows angled. Releasing a quick yawn, he looked at his nails, looking bored.

"There are no monsters here. You seek what cannot be found." Spreading his arms, he looked from left to right. "And who am I, you ask? 'Tis a mystery, is it not?" Then his eyes blazed in mystification. "How did you climb the mountain?"

Jack scoffed and said with a wicked tone, "'Tis a mystery, is it not?"

The man's body hardened and his eyes drilled Jack with fury.

I stepped out of Jack's shadow and waved my own dagger. "Who are those people? Why are they hurt? What curse have you placed upon them?"

Giving me a sideways glance, he spread his lips wide. I did not like his smile. I assumed he had something wicked in mind.

"I did nothing to them."

He sounded sincere.

"'Twas not I, but rather your God. I'd not hurt you. Put your daggers down and meet my people."

Jack and I exchanged wary glances, silently asking each other what we should do. When I shrugged and started to follow the scarred man, Jack tailed behind me. I needed answers, and only the man could give them.

Out in the open cavern, the sun's rays shone like a spring day, but no warmth lay upon the people—only evil and darkness, I was sure of it. The men waited, watching us without a sound, while we stood at the higher end of the cave, so his people had a clear view of us.

"Meet my family." He offered a genuine smile and looked upon his people like a proud father to his children.

As I glanced over the crowd, I saw no horrendous wounds. Whole and unharmed, these men—bare-chested with tattered breeches—looked content and healthy. But they did not speak.

Horror tugged at my gut and eerie dread held me prisoner.

Jack clapped his hands once hard, startling the scarred man. "Excellent. It was pleasant to meet your people. It was ... how should I say this? Not nice to meet you. It's time for us to leave. How about you let *our* people go?"

The scarred man's eyes turned a shade darker. "I am not finished." He growled and then softened his tone. "Come, sit and have a meal with me." He proceeded to the table.

"No," I said. "You have ears to hear, my friend. We shall go."

"I do not take no for an answer, little girl. If you refuse to sit and eat with me, there shall be consequences. One of your people will lose an arm," he said calmly, as if the words were not threatening.

When he jerked his head sideways, a group of men gathered behind us. They outnumbered us ten to two. Having no choice, I pulled out the wooden worn chair and sat across from him.

One of your people will lose an arm.

What kind of monster was he? Warning chills pricked my nape, and every one of my senses told me to run. *Run. Run. Run.*

A display of mouthwatering food spread over the table like the day before. The scarred man placed dirty wooden plates in front of us, the remains of someone else's meal still clinging to them. He did not provide utensils.

"Please, have whatever your heart desires." He sat back down and grabbed a slab of meat, cheese, and carrots for his plate.

I craned my neck to peek at his people, who went about unremarkable tasks—attending the sheep, harvesting, planting vegetables where the sun shone brightest. Some were getting water from the stream with buckets and watering the vegetation. I was glad they weren't still staring at us.

"Do your people partake of this food they grow?" I contained my fear and eyed the food I wanted to eat, but dared not touch.

He smiled, chewing with his mouth open. "You care about my people. It pleases me, but do not worry your heart. As long as I eat, they are full."

What does he mean?

I folded my hands in my lap to keep steady. "Why are our people your prisoners?"

I did not dare mention one of the men was my father. I did not want him to use that against me.

The scarred man bit into his meat and licked his fingers. "Your people killed one of mine."

"But they killed a monster, not a man," I said.

"Exactly. But they are not monsters, I assure you."

His words confused me, but I carried on. "They did right by killing one of the beasts. How many are there? Where do they live? And why are you here?" So many unanswered questions swam in my head. "Please. Do you have the key to the cage? Please help me release the prisoners." Then an ugly thought entered my mind.

Perhaps he helped the monsters? Maybe he fed them people and sheep. He had plenty of both. "Why do you have so many sheep? You stole them from my people, did you not?"

The scarred man waved a chunk of meat as if annoyed by me. "You have a bundle of questions I do not wish to answer."

"Then let us be." I huffed out a breath as my fingernails dug into the crack of the wooden chair.

I gave Jack the evil eye when he took a bite of cooked meat. He froze, glared back and dropped it to his plate. Jack had better have a plan, or at least be thinking of one instead of filling his thoughts with the meal.

"I'm afraid I cannot do as you ask."

His composed tone made the anger in me scorch hotter. I slammed my hand on the table so hard, everything on it jumped. My palm stung, the pain rattled up my arm and to my bones, but I had no care.

"Why not? If you do not let us go, then *you* are the monster."

The scarred man leapt out of his seat, eyes furious and his muscles like rock. Jack's chair fell back when he stood in haste. He held his dagger out, preventing the scarred man from coming for me.

"Do not lay your filthy hands on her. Keep your hands filled with your meal." Jack sneered. "So help me God, I'll kill you. Give us answers fast before I lose my patience. My brothers are coming with our people. They're already on their way. If we're not out, there'll be bloodshed. Your people don't look fit for battle."

The scarred man scowled, sat back down, and picked up a piece of bread. "Do you know the story about Jesus and the centurion with the lance?"

"Aye, but 'tis not a story. 'Tis in the Bible," Jack said. "Why do you speak of the holy book?"

The scarred man ignored Jack and peered up after breaking his bread into two pieces. "Take this and eat it, for this is my body."

He held out a piece of bread, which I did not take.

He scoffed. "You know the story of this man who pierced Jesus's side to ensure his death? He did what he was told, his duty. How could he have known Jesus was the son of God?" He paused. "I'm going to tell you what's missing from the Bible. The part they dared not put in. Hypocrites."

Jack and I glanced at each other. I knew he was thinking the same as I when he tapped his head. This man had gone beyond mad. But we had no choice but to listen.

"Carry on." Jack scowled, picked up the fallen chair and sat next to me. "I can't wait to hear this story."

The scarred man glared, and then softened his eyes. "Three women witnessed the man with the lance piercing Jesus's side: Jesus's mother, Mary, the mother of the sons of Zebedee, and Mary Magdalene. What happened after was a mystery. Again, the man was just following orders. Mary Magdalene cursed the man with the lance, and then she cursed every man in Golgotha, the hill where they crucified your Jesus. I understood her pain, anger, and wanting revenge, but she went too far."

"The soldier deserved it, but maybe not the other people who did not know who Jesus was," I said. "However, I'm sure the curse compared nothing to what she felt."

Surprisingly, the man did not counter. Instead, he looked

somber and took a long sip from his cup. Some drops dribbled down his chin, red like blood, and he wiped them with the back of his hand.

"But it did," he finally said. "Mary Magdalene cursed them to eternal damnation. On the night of the curse, the people suffered vicious attacks from invisible forces, as though a lion mauled them from head to toe until the sun rose. They started to heal at dawn and healed for days. When they were well and back to themselves, the cycle started again. Do you think those people deserved such suffering?"

I did not want anyone to suffer, but I did not speak, in case he told false tales. Jack bowed his head, and I assumed he pitied the imagined people's anguish, as I did.

"No, they do not," the man said softly. "Not at all. Not only did the people suffer as if demons ate their flesh and bone, but on those nights, they became the monsters of scary bedtime stories. They grow three times taller, and hair like a lion's spread over every inch of their bodies. The bones in their hands and feet break and reform into paws with long, sharp claws. Their broken jaws and cheekbones take shape on a hideous face—half-human and half-beast. And their teeth grow long and razor sharp. How was this a fair punishment? Dying and being sent to Hell might have been better."

Taller than life ... claws like a beast ... teeth as sharp as knives.

He seemed to believe he was telling us a true tale, not a bedtime story. I listened and kept my senses alert. I knew, somehow, I could use his story to my advantage. I had to use my wits, but how?

And then—Jack. Stupid, hare brained Jack.

"'Tis a good story. Lies, but good story indeed." Jack moved to the edge of his seat, pulling on my cape. "Thank you for the entertainment, but we must go." He pointed up. "The day certainly seemed to speed by."

The scarred man growled like a wild beast and pounded once on the table. "I am not finished."

I stilled, and silence reigned.

"Now, where did I…" He paused for a moment and proceeded with a calmer tone. "Because of their transformation, the man with the lance led his people on a long journey, as far as they could go from the place of the curse. They hid in a mountain. To protect themselves from people who seek to kill them, they tore down the trees on the mountain and salted the earth to ensure the surface could not be climbed. People called this place the Black Mountain because of its color." He paused, staring into the rocky wall, as if to recall his past. Cocking an eyebrow, he bore his eyes to mine. "How did you climb the mountain no man has ever climbed before?"

When I didn't answer, he snarled.

"I'll find out soon enough. Now, back to the story. They tried to stay hidden, but one problem always remained. To heal the cursed wounds and stay human on other nights, they needed to sacrifice a sheep during each cycle of their changing. And the man who wielded the lance needed to drink a cup of the sheep's blood."

I glanced at the flock of sheep and the hair rose on the back of my neck. If he and his people were truly the people of the tale, then the sheep being there made sense and explained why nearby towns had lost their flocks.

These people stole sheep for the monsters they became? And the horrible injuries of the people had healed. I'd seen it with my own eyes.

Then I gazed upon the people with a somber heart. What must it be like for them to go through such a torturous curse? Did they know what had been done to them? And if they did, had they renounced God in their hearts? Certainly, they acted as though they had no opinion. Or did they fear the scarred man.

"How often does this happen?" I asked.

A wave of unwanted feelings rose in my throat as I pieced what I had heard and experienced together: the vision of the monster when I'd touched Father's lance; the cries only I had heard; and the image of this scarred man.

As I sorted the thoughts in my mind, my pulse raced like a galloping horse. His story intrigued me. I needed answers about the painful cries I'd heard so many nights.

"It comes and goes when it's time. It's a cruel and unjust punishment. The centurion didn't hammer the nails through Jesus on the cross. This man did not order the crucifixion. He only checked to make sure the prisoners were dead. It was the task assigned to him for every man who was crucified."

Jack released a long sigh. "Liar. You've gone mad and sold your soul to the devil." He stood again.

"What I speak is true." He rounded his fists on the table, as if to give us a warning.

"Blasphemy. You keep these people prisoner here for some evil purpose of your own. If what you say is true, where is the proof?" Jack's voice grew louder with each word.

The scarred man tipped over his cup and jerked his head up as his nostrils flared. Lines creased his forehead and his body shook with rage. Crimson liquid pooled on the table, too thick to be wine, and dripped between the cracks to the floor.

Breath left me in a gasp.

Still glaring at us, he announced with conviction, "This is the blood of the sacrificed lamb, and I am that man!"

Chapter Fourteen

Longinus

rip. Drip. Drip.

I held my breath. Silence filled the cave, except for the sound of blood falling to the cave floor. Even his people stood still, watching in silence.

"I am the man who stabbed Jesus as he took his last breath. My name is Longinus."

Jack pulled me out of my chair, gripping my arm. With a trembling hand, he pointed his dagger at Longinus. "Release the prisoners and I'll keep my people away. We won't bother you again. You can live in peace with your people and the monsters."

Longinus's chest rose and fell with a sigh. "I tried being nice, but you're not being grateful. Your people took a life, and now I must take one of theirs."

"Blasphemer. What in God's name do you mean?" Jack roared. His eyes smoldered with anger. "You killed two of our people."

"They died in a battle they began. My men captured the other three. One must face the same fate. You may choose who will die and who will live. Life for a life."

"No," I said. "We can strike a bargain."

"Men?" Jack blinked in surprise. "Your people are not men. They are monsters."

Longinus shook his head. "Have you not heard anything I've said? Your ignorance will save you no more." He turned to a few men near him and pointed to us. "Get them."

"Well done, Jack." Pulling away from him, I yanked a dagger from my boot.

I stood back to back with Jack, waving my dagger from side to side. The men surrounding us were not fit for battle. They had no swords or daggers, but they came at us with strength. When I nicked one on the chest, he backed away. Jack shoved another fellow, who stumbled back and fell atop other men.

"Stop. I do not want to hurt you." My dagger shook in my hand.

Father and I had practiced sword fighting, but this was different. The fight was real, and blood would be shed by my hand. I had never wanted to kill a being, human or animal, but that day might have come.

One brave soul jumped for me, and I cut his arm, just enough to hurt him. I cringed when he shrieked in pain. Then the scenario took a turn for the worse when Jack stabbed a few men who rushed at him. The others roared and scrambled away. Hurting the unarmed men was nothing to be proud of, and I felt sorry for them.

"Cease this nonsense."

When I turned in the direction of Longinus's booming voice, my thundering heart stopped. Father and his friends stood next to Longinus. Each of them had a dagger pressed to their necks, held by Longinus's men.

"Father." I realized too late I'd made a mistake.

Longinus looked at me and then to my father. His wicked grin widened. I bowed my head in regret.

"Come here, girl," Longinus said.

Longinus had Father and his friends, so I had no choice. I placed my dagger back inside my boot, and Jack followed.

"No, not you." Longinus shook his head. "Put your dagger down."

Jack scowled and did as told. "Let her go."

If Jack had any wit, he would not attack. He had to think about his father too.

Longinus watched me stumble toward him with a triumphant grin. "I haven't had this much fun in, well ... I've never had this much fun. For so many years, I've been alone."

"You have your people. Play your tricks on them. What do they think of your lies?"

Longinus's eyes glowed like the devil's when Jack mocked him with his words. "For every word from your wicked tongue, I'll cut her with her own dagger."

He pulled it out of my boot as the two men beside me held my arms wide. Blood drained from my face and my legs buckled.

"Stop. Forgive my insults. Or wound me instead."

Longinus paid no mind to Jack's apology. When Jack tried to reach for me, Longinus's men held him back. After Longinus untied my cloak, it pooled around my boots.

"Roll up her sleeve," he said to the men holding me.

In spite of myself, I looked to Father.

Father's eyes rounded in fear, and he struggled against his captors. "Please. I beg you. I'll do anything you ask. I can give you coins, land, sheep, what your heart desires. Let her go. She's just a child. Have mercy. Please have mercy on her."

Guilt would become his demon, for he could not save his only child, his most precious thing. He would have to watch me die. I had never seen my father cry. His tears made mine fall as well. He broke my heart as I did his.

Longinus made no answer to Father and stood behind me. "You are vulnerable. I have been, too, all these centuries."

His breath burned hot on my neck. My skin pricked when the dagger's cold blade pressed against my throat, teasing me. Then he walked around to face me and placed the tip of the dagger under my chin and lifted my head.

A tiny whimper escaped my mouth.

Longinus grazed the blade lower and pierced the side of my neck. Pain shot down my spine. I bit my lip from crying out as warm liquid seeped down.

"Stop." Jack took a step, but Longinus's men gathered around him.

Longinus cut to Jack with cold steel eyes, then easily dismissed him. "I begged and pleaded every cycle for the curse to stop. Not just for me, but for my people. My prayers were never answered. God had no mercy on me or these people. What kind of God turns away prayers from those who are suffering?"

At first I'd pitied him, but I wanted to spit in his face for his cruelty. "God only hears prayers that deserve to be answered. You are not worthy."

The words tumbled without thought to my tongue, but I hoped I made him feel small and loathsome.

"Does He now?" Longinus's face inched closer to mine.

Staring at the freckles on his nose, I breathed in his scent. For someone who had been cursed for life, he did not smell bad. A cursed person should smell like rotting fish to proclaim their evil.

Longinus would have had a handsome face if he hadn't been possessed by malice. His beautiful midnight blue eyes softened when they met mine. Then he took a step back, his irises darkened like night falling, and his shoulders tensed.

"Tell me, little girl, will your God hear your prayers when I cut you?" He dragged the dagger across my shoulder. "Your blood will spill on this floor and your soul will break. And I will rejoice to see you renounce your God and kneel before me as you die."

I pushed back hard, but the men held me firm. What could I say or do to sway him? I could not stand there mute; I had to fight for my life.

"Why would you do such a thing? You want me to believe you are undeserving of your fate. Prove it. Killing me will not change the past. Seek not revenge. You will only hurt yourself and your people." My voice rose to echo off the cavern walls. "Repent of your sins, and you shall find salvation."

Longinus blinked. Tilting his head, he stared at me as if he were seeing me for the first time. "I have not sinned. I did no wrong. I am a good man. My purpose is to save you. Mary cursed me to suffer for eternity. *Mary* has sinned, not I. Now I speak the words Mary spoke to me before she cursed me. Repent of your sins, and *you* shall find salvation." Then he slashed my forearm with the dagger.

I screamed in pain as blood splashed beneath me, painting the dirt with crimson.

"Stop! Please." Father bucked against the men holding him. "Please. Let me take her place."

"You have a caring father," Longinus said.

His compliment seemed odd at the moment.

My tongue twisted in knots, and pain took my mind. I bit my bottom lip to keep from screaming again.

Longinus ran his fingers through my hair and yanked my head back. "You're a brave soul … for now. I've just begun. Prepare yourself."

"You coward. Why not hurt someone your own size?" Jack shoved the men around him, but there were too many.

Longinus looked over his shoulder to Jack and hissed. "It is not about size, you fool."

"You are no man."

"I am not merely a man, I assure you. I will be the end of your world and the beginning of a new one when I claim your land. Centuries of hiding didn't protect my people, so I will free them and take back what was once mine."

"Name your price," Jack said, panic struck in his eyes. "Take me. I beg you let her be."

Jack's pleading surprised me. I thought he would run and save himself. His chivalry softened my heart.

"Dust thou art, and unto dust shalt thou return." Longinus sliced twice across my arm near my wrist.

I wanted to scream to relieve the agony, but the pain took my voice. Blood spilled from the deep cuts into small puddles on the ground. My pulse raced, my heart drummed faster. Every inch of my body burned like I had caught fire.

Father struggled to get loose, his mouth opened with his own silent scream. The pain in his eyes was palpable. "Please, please, please."

The cave spun in circles. I was too young to die. I would never know life to the fullest. If Father somehow survived, which I doubted, he would be daughterless and blame himself for eternity.

For a moment, as Jack and I locked eyes, I pictured us wed and my belly full with his child. Such silly visions would never come to be, but imagining a future comforted me. It helped me focus on something besides the pain.

But the pain ... so real ... such torture ... the devil's touch.

I convulsed from the ache, no longer able to bear it. As Longinus cut me again on the left arm, my right arm ceased to feel the scorching sensation. A bright light shone down on me from above, giving me warmth and peace and comfort.

People said when death neared a divine light would lead the way.

Am I to leave this world?

The way Jack stared at me with wide eyes, he must have known my last breath rattled in my chest.

Longinus dropped his arm and backed away fearfully. Clenching his hair in a fist, he stared hard at me. The pain faded completely, and I gazed at my right arm—healed. I looked to my left arm—healed. No evidence of Longinus's torture remained, just the blood from previous slashes.

What in God's name? Did an angel save me? What just happened?

When the lance had cut me, though a smaller wound, it had healed quickly. I tried to think to childhood. I'd never thought to watch how fast my wounds healed. I had no playmates with whom to compare skinned knees.

I glanced between Father, Jack, Longinus, and even the men holding me, searching for proof they had seen the same. Their slack faces spoke for them.

Holy Jesus.

"Impossible." Longinus gawked in places he had wounded me. "You will not die? After all these centuries, finally one of Mary's descendants has found me? Were you born with…?"

Longinus sniffed me and then took a step back. He observed me for few long seconds, his expression unreadable. Then he lunged forward, grabbed my wrist, and studied the birthmark. He rubbed it with his finger, and then checked the other wrist holding both up in front of my face.

"These are birthmarks?" Longinus asked.

"No." I yanked my arms back as the lie escaped my mouth.

Longinus strode to my father and pressed the dagger against his face hard enough to draw blood. "Tell me, father of the girl. Was she born with those marks?"

Father gave him wicked eyes and would not answer.

"Tell me." Longinus lowered the dagger to my father's neck and nicked him.

Blood trickled down Father's throat. Longinus's muscles tensed for a strike.

"Aye." If Father would not save himself, I must. "'Tis true. These marks have been with me since birth."

Longinus came back to me. "Tell me little girl, do you bear marks on your feet?"

117

I nodded.

"Stigmata." My dagger wavered in his hand as he pointed it at me, mumbling a sort of recited chant. "'For your sin, you shall suffer for eternity. Repent. Then only shall you find salvation. I leveled the curse because of Christ, my descendants carry the marks. Those of my bloodline who bear the stigmata can break the curse. This I offer to you once.'" He then slowly peered up at me with cold, evil, calculating eyes.

I shivered.

"Mary, Mary, Mary, I remember your words of damnation." He started to circle me. "You have sent me your bloodline, but I won't take it. You are dead, but I live. I will live for eternity, thanks to you. You think me a fool? You sent this girl to end my life, when all I have taken are sheep to ease our suffering? For this, I will punish your people as you have done to mine for these ages. Let us see if your people can face the monsters."

I gasped, hoping it only to be a threat, but I knew better.

He lifted his chin with satisfaction. "Take these men back to their cell." He turned to his people. "When we are beasts, we shall take what is ours. We will hunt humans, not sheep. I will be the end of your world and the beginning of a new one when I claim your land. I will be God!"

The loud roars and the thunderous stomping from his people shook the mountain.

God have mercy on us all.

Chapter Fifteen
Oh, Jack

If Longinus spoke the truth, then I was born of Mary Magdalene's bloodline through one of my parents. My heart held many questions, but I was afraid some questions would remain unanswered.

Father and his friends went back to their prison, and Longinus's men tossed Jack and me into another. I pushed my sleeve down after smearing the remaining blood on my tunic, ashamed as though my odd markings made me a monster, too.

Drained, and bile rising in my throat, I huddled in a corner. The damp cave chilled me, and the pungent odor of something foul turned my stomach. I gagged.

"Are you well?" Jack leaned against the rocky wall.

For the first time, he seemed to lack fancy words, and his arrogance had gone. I thought he would ask me a bundle of questions, but thankfully he did not.

"I am well." I rolled my eyes. "Look around you. 'Tis pleasant here in this princess's chamber. Plenty of food. Smells like a rose garden. I love being imprisoned and learning I'm some kind of abomination with unnatural powers." I rubbed my arm, remembering the pain as Longinus had sliced my flesh.

Jack sat next to me on the musty hay. He tilted my chin up

and brushed my hair back. "Jacky. You're not an abomination. You're a miracle. I do not know what you did, but I saw Heaven's light. Glorious, I tell you, like a kiss from God. It was beautiful, hypnotizing to the eyes, just like you."

I stared into his beautiful green eyes, utterly distracted as he stared into mine. Surely, he meant to make me feel better. However, knowing his reputation for flattery, I did not take his compliment to heart. I appreciated his kindness, but nothing could grant me peace until we were all free and safe.

"We must find a way to escape." Jack broke the awkwardness between us.

For a moment I thought he leaned closer to kiss me, like the Jack I'd known before, but he did not.

"I'm beaten. I see no way to leave here." My words parted from me with exhaustion. Though my wounds had healed, the torture left me drained. "I hope you have some clever idea."

He did not answer me. Instead, he asked softly, "You want to talk about what happened?"

I bit my lip. I'd hoped Jack would avoid that question. How could I answer when I did not even know?

"Jaclyn." My father's voice called me away from Jack.

Grateful for the interruption, I ran to the corner nearest his prison.

"Father," I whispered. "Are you well?"

He reached to me through the space between our cells. As soon as I touched his fingers, tears rolled down my face. I needed more of him. I needed his arms around me, the way he had comforted me when I had been a little girl.

Those simple acts of love were rare when life became so busy. I took time for granted. My heart heavy, I folded my arms to steady myself against a lake of tears.

"How can you ask if I am well when you, my child, were wounded by the monster?" Father asked after a long stretch of silence. "Are you in pain?"

I wiped my tears. "I am confused. I cannot believe my eyes. It is like a dream. Can Longinus's words be true? Mary Magdalene's blood lies within you or Mother? And why did you not tell me?"

Father made a strange noise and cleared his throat. "Jaclyn, your mother and I planned to tell you someday, together. Not this way. You have the right to know, especially after what has happened today. Please know your mother and I love you very much. We meant to tell you."

My stomach clenched. Whatever he had to tell me, I sensed it would pain me to hear it.

"What is it, Father?" My fists held fast on the wooden poles keeping me in, and I prepared myself.

"Your mother wanted to bear children for years, but she could not. Then one day, a pounding at our front door woke me in the middle of a cold night. When I opened the door, a basket and a lance awaited. To my surprise, when I brought the basket in, I found a baby inside. You were so small and beautiful. We hid you from the outside world. When it got difficult, we moved to the farm. The monsters' cries at night had begun and scared the townspeople so badly the entire town prepared to move. It was a perfect disguise for our secret.

"We told everyone you were a miracle and raised you as our

own. We knew you were special. Your birthmarks could only mean you were blessed by God. We do not know the meaning of the lance you arrived with, but I kept it safe, hidden away. We thought maybe one day your mother would claim you, but no one came. Never did a day pass we did not love you like our own. For us, you *are* our own. I sincerely apologize for withholding the truth, but we hoped to protect you from whatever mystery brought you to us. Can you forgive us?"

My mind wheeled back to touching the lance, and I saw again the man and the monster he masked. Why the lance, and what did it mean? What was God's will? I did not know.

Father's cry for forgiveness pierced my heart. My vision blurred, and I could not wipe the falling tears away fast enough. How I wished we could be in the same prison.

"There's nothing to forgive. You will always be my father. You cared for me, showed me how to be strong, fed me, and taught me love is precious. What you show me is love can be given freely, unconditionally. You love me not because you brought me into this world, but because your heart is good and kind. You chose to give me your pure love, the best kind of all. I was sent to you because you are deserving and I'm honored to be your daughter."

The cave echoed with clapping, and Longinus stepped out of the shadows. "How touching. Now I know the truth. Too bad your father is not of Mary's blood. Your father will not heal himself when my monsters rip him apart. However, little girl, you can join our family. We are of the same coin."

"Nay, I am not like you." Holding on to the pole, I rattled it with all my strength. "The townspeople will come for you. They'll find you and your people if you don't let us go. Do you hear me?" My voice rang against the walls of the caves and reverberated to the stream.

Jack placed his arms around me and pulled me away, but I pushed him and went back to the bars. Out of breath, I stared coldly at Longinus.

He stared back, his eyes different this time, a bit scared perhaps. Scared or not, it didn't matter. He would break me and kill us all.

He finally spoke. "Where are these people of yours?" He tapped his head with a finger. "I think they're not coming. You see, people are afraid of the unknown. They fear death even more. Don't worry, little girl. I'll let you out when my people are ready to hunt. The monsters will find them all. We will rip through town after town, until my revenge has been satisfied. Do not waste your breath in prayer. God has forsaken you." With an evil grin, he walked away.

It took every ounce of my patience not to slam my body against the poles. I would only hurt myself, but my rage dared me to try. As I shoved my face against the bars, I pressed harder with each word. Though Longinus continued to walk away, I needed to say what I felt in my heart.

"The devil's blood pumps through your heart, friend. You deserve every evil thing that has and will happen to you."

"Rest yourself, Jacky. You will need all your strength."

I spun around to see Jack lying comfortably on the ground with a piece of hay in his mouth as if he had not a care in the world.

"I do not wish to be called Jacky." I pressed my back to the poles and dug my heels into the dirt.

"I apologize, Jaclyn. All will be fine." He patted the ground next to him and waggled a finger at me. "Come hither. I shall keep you warm."

I crinkled my nose and narrowed my eyes at him.

How can he be so playful at a time like this?

Some people dealt danger with humor to help them not to lose their mind.

My cloak lay still on the ground where Longinus had cut me. I didn't miss it until Jack mentioned keeping me warm. I had rather hug a pig than let Jack warm me. Although, I hated to admit he looked appealing with his arms behind his neck, muscles filling his tunic in an alluring way. Uncomfortable heat poured through me again.

These feelings must be more of Longinus's tricks.

"How could you say all will be well? We're locked in here."

"You're right. We are. Let us pass the time pleasantly."

"You're unbearable." I ran my hand down my face and sighed in frustration. "You are the last person I want to embrace."

"Who said anything about embracing? I think more like I'll rub your feet and then you rub mine to thank me."

I blinked rapidly, astounded. "Eh? Thank you for what?"

He reached inside his boot and pulled out a small, dangling object. "For this." His lips spread smugly, his eyes glistening. "I stole the key from the guard when he threw us in here."

My lips slowly lifted into a playful smile. "You're brilliant. And clearly, your criminal nature is a boon to us."

"We'll make our way out when everyone is asleep. Now, how about a kiss?"

I shook my head and rolled my eyes.

I wanted to tell Father, but Longinus or his men would be watching us. Jack probably wanted to let his father know as well, but it was safer to keep it between us until it was time.

"Perhaps you will lend me your cloak like a gentleman?" I smirked, thinking he would not refuse.

"Perhaps you can come here and get it?"

There was so much playfulness in his tone. Something warm kindled inside me and grew with every step I took toward him. If he thought I'd succumb to his charms, he'd better think twice.

I knew how to bring down a man.

Chapter Sixteen

Escape

Relenting, because there was nowhere else to go, I slumped next to Jack. As time passed, the sunlight disappeared and lights from the lanterns and candles took its place. The cave seemed exceptionally bright that evening.

I stirred when footsteps pounded on dirt. Expecting Longinus, I sat taller, but one of his men appeared instead. He slipped two plates of food and a cup of water under the bar and left.

Jack picked it up and set it in front of me. Bread and cooked meat, probably mutton, filled the plate. I pushed it aside, bent my knees to my chest, and laid down my head.

"Jaclyn, you must eat. You'll need your strength tonight."

When I refused to eat, Jack tried to feed me, but I turned away. He gave up and ate, chewing vigorously and sucking loudly on his fingers. Watching him made my stomach rumble. He made eating look so good. I laughed despite our ill-fated state.

"Jaclyn." My father's voice echoed into my prison. "Please eat your meal. You must keep up your strength."

Father always worried about me. It did not matter he was locked up. It did not matter he could not see. I was always on his mind. I wished I could be with him.

I leaned against the pole. "Don't worry."

"If you do not eat, I will not eat. Jack will let me know if you speak the truth."

"Aye, Father."

I sighed and picked up my plate. In truth, I did not want to eat anything Longinus gave me.

My mind turned over thoughts of escape alongside questions about my true parents. Using my fingers, I scooped up meat and chewed. The first bite tasted cold, but satisfying, and I finished my meal quickly.

"And how shall we escape?" I asked Jack.

He leaned closer. So close, heat rose to my face and traveled down to my toes.

"We leave when everyone is asleep. We'll pretend to be asleep, too."

"Then what?"

"I'll unlock the doors with the key. We'll move slowly and carefully."

"What if someone wakes up? What if they do not sleep at all?"

"Then we run."

"That's it?" My tone sharpened.

"Shhh." He placed a finger against my mouth.

His touch left me tingling. I liked how it made me feel, warmth prickling through my veins, but I pushed his hand away.

Jack draped his cloak over me, then he lay down, stretching out. "You will see. It will work. Sometimes you can't prepare. You must take opportunities as they arise."

I had no idea what would happen when we got out, but first things first, I wanted my dagger.

"Where might Longinus keep our weapons? Do you know where to look?"

Jack would not have a clue, but I thought I'd ask.

"I do. They are placed next to the treasure."

"Treasure?" I inched my body closer to his. "You found treasure? Where? And how do you know?"

"What do I get if I tell you?" he asked with an insolent grin.

I frowned. "I'll put my fist in your face if you don't tell. That's what you'll get."

Though I hated to admit it, his teasing kept my mind off Longinus. And I loved to tease back.

Jack let out a laugh. "You're not nice to your hero."

He sounded insulted, though I doubted he had the sense to be. Crossing his legs, he turned his bottom lip into a pout.

"Hero? What makes you think you're my hero?"

"I'm going to save you, take you out of here. 'Tis my promise to you."

I wished Jack could see the future, to let me know all would be fine. I hoped he would be my hero and take us home.

"Why do you care if I live or die? What am I to you?"

Jack placed his hand over his heart. "I'm hurt. We've been friends since our younger days. Of course I care about you. And you're going to be my wife."

My face turned red-hot like the cooking fire. I spun around so he could not see my smile. I'd never known a boy as appealing as Jack, but I would not let him know.

I raised my head and met his eyes boldly. "You didn't answer my previous question. How do you know about the treasure?"

He smiled, that wicked, mischievous smile. "I wandered about while you were sleeping behind the boulder. I like to be aware of my surroundings. Find the threats and possible exits."

My anger rose and my cheeks burned. "You knew where I was and you didn't ... You didn't..."

I stopped and turned my back to him when I realized my voice echoed loudly in our cell. His behavior was no cause for alarm. Wasting my breath for something petty was a misuse of time and effort. Instead, I let out a long sigh. There were more pressing matters at hand.

The flickering candlelight reminded me the sun had set, and the quiet told me the people were asleep. It was almost time.

While Jack went to the far right of the prison to speak to his father, I sat by the lock and stared at it. All seemed so peaceful and quiet, but danger lay beyond the prison, and we meant to go right through the middle of it. I prayed we would all escape in one piece.

I must have dozed off. My eyes flashed open and my hands covered my ears to block the sounds of tortured cries. Curling my knees in to my chest, I moaned. It happened again—screams echoed in my head. I hummed my mother's tune. With my eyes shut, I tried to drown out the sounds, but like always, it did not work.

"Jaclyn, are you hurt?"

I faintly heard Jack's voice, as if he covered his mouth while he spoke.

"It's too loud. I hear their cries." I didn't know how loud or soft I spoke. No one knew of my secret nightmares, but I felt I had no choice but to tell Jack.

"I know. Something's happening."

I tilted my head to meet his gaze. "You heard them?"

The question had been answered. More screams tore through the night from the direction of the cavern. The same sound echoed both inside my head and outside it. Somehow, the monsters and I were one.

"It's time." Jack helped me to my feet. "I'm getting us out of here. We're not sitting around to be a monster's meal. Who knows how many there are?"

Jack wove his arm through the bars, opened the lock, and pushed the door. Then he went to our fathers' prison and unlocked it.

William pulled Jack into his arms. "Well done, my son. Lead us out of here."

Father stepped around William to embrace me. Warmth, love, and security enveloped me, and I let out a sigh of relief, but it lasted only a few seconds. We weren't out of danger yet. We'd just begun.

"I'm so sorry, Jaclyn," my father said, his features twisted in sorrow.

I knew the reason for his apology, but it wasn't the time to speak of it. "Nay, Father. Let us talk when we are safe."

He nodded in agreement, pulling away.

"We must go now." Jack led the way toward the light and the horrid sound.

When the first gleams fell on the tortured souls, my lips parted as I watched in horror. Jack and the men behind me stood still, quiet, and afraid. As the men bent and screamed in pain, the hair on their heads and bodies grew and coarsened.

Their frames stretched, tearing the fabric of their breeches. Sharp claws sprouted from their fingers and toes. Their faces transformed as their jaws expanded and thrust forward. Teeth jutted out sharply, growing ten times in size. They tossed about, crying out in agony. I had no words to describe what they looked like between human and beast.

"Holy Mother of God. This is the work of the devil," John murmured under his breath, looking horrified.

"Come." Jack broke us out of the trance. "We need to get out before they're changed fully."

"I need my sword." Father adjusted his hat.

"I agree, we'd have a better chance making it back with our weapons," William said.

Jack pointed to the darkness. "Our swords are where the treasure is. This way."

He led us to the back of the cave, from where the stream flowed. The lantern's glow revealed vibrant flowers I would have never imagined inside a cavern.

Moss covered the ground, even the trunks of the trees. Tangled lush vines adorned the walls. It looked more like a garden in a fairytale setting. And in the middle, a pile of gold coins and all sorts of jewelry mounted to the ceiling. Lights from the cracks illuminated the treasures. A magnificent sight. Off to the side were our daggers and swords.

"Quickly." Jack dashed.

After I grabbed my weapon, my greedy eyes strayed to the countless precious stones—diamonds, sapphires, rubies, and emeralds—of various sizes on the way out. Then I shifted my attention to a piece of brown material and picked up my cloak.

I gave Jack back his cloak, swung mine around my shoulders and tied it to keep it in place.

"No." My father placed his hand over John's and closed it into a fist.

John had picked up some gold coins.

"We don't steal. This is the devil's money. No good will come from it."

John scowled and yanked his hand back.

Jack raised his hand to stop us. "Listen."

I froze.

"Do you hear that?" Jack asked. "The sounds are diminishing. We need to leave now."

I trailed Jack and stopped at the mouth of the tunnel. Some men had fully turned to monsters and stared at us like their next meal.

"Run," Father said. "This way."

A loud roar thundered and vibrated against the wall. One of the monsters, taller and bigger than the others, stood in our way. It must have been Longinus.

I ran in the opposite direction behind Father, finding my way and weaving around the other beasts coming for me. They were the kind of beasts parents told their children about so they would behave. But this was no bedtime story. They had scared me senseless when I'd first seen them capture Father, but so many of them—no words could describe the moment.

My muscles did not want to obey, and my movements became stiff. I found the strength to be brave from the men around me.

Trained for battle, they moved with purpose.

"This way." Jack took the lead as he slid down a slope inside the tunnel.

I had to go the opposite way, since monsters blocked my escape.

"There are too many of them." William sliced his sword across a monster's legs.

It bellowed in pain and dropped to the ground. Its cry carried throughout the cave, drawing more to us.

The monsters being three times my size, I was able to hide between their legs, sometimes running under them. Their long arms and claws lifted the dirt and pebbles as they tried to grab me, causing dust to cloud my vision.

After I stabbed one in the foot, I ran across to another monster and did the same. I wished to shove the dagger through a head or heart, but they were taller than life—giants.

Jack moved with skill and grace in unexpected ways. Some might say he was crazy, but I thought he was smart and courageous. Jack gripped a handful of one monster's belly hair, swung around, and landed on the monster's shoulder as if he were a tumbler entertaining crowds at the market. His dagger penetrated the monster's neck, and the creature screeched as blood gushed down its body. Jack jumped off just before the monster fell on top of other monsters and knocked them down.

The beasts' large size hampered them; having to bend lower to try to catch us affected their coordination. However, the thunder of their fierce stomping caused pebbles and rocks to fall. They scraped their claws along the wall, collapsing more debris around us.

Father tried to stay close to me as I dodged legs and claws and rocks, but it was nearly impossible. Jack also stayed close by as if to protect me. Despite their care, one small boulder crashed down into my back, slamming me sideways against the wall.

Darkness engulfed me.

When I blinked my eyes open, my vision blurred, the cave spun, and the silhouettes of the monsters lingered. Father's mouth moved, but no sound escaped.

Darkness took me again, but I must have recovered quickly. I found myself still prone in my father's arms, while Jack and the others threatened the monsters with their swords and daggers.

"Jaclyn, can you move?" Father shook me lightly.

Ignoring him, I stood and planted my hand on the wall for support, despite my head throbbing and body protesting. Something wet on the side of my temple caught my attention. When I wiped it, scarlet liquid smeared my fingers.

"She's up. Let's go," Father said.

Then I took off again, racing across the rope bridge.

"I think we need to go in different directions to confuse the monsters," William said. "Jack, John, and I will go this way." He pointed to the left.

"Meet us at the bottom of the mountain. Godspeed." Father took my hand and we ran, causing chaos for the monsters, as they did not know who to follow.

"There, Father." I pointed ahead. "I see the moon. It's our way out."

Relief burst through my marrow as the familiar icy air chilled me. My heart hammered joyfully too soon when I ran out of the cave. I screamed as flames blocked the path to the beanstalk—hissing and crackling.

No one knew of the beanstalk except for Jack and me. Climbing down the mountain was not an option. And I knew Longinus had caused the fire when he climbed onto an oversized boulder with a torch.

I tugged Father toward the beanstalk, but became confused by the rapid growing blaze. Unable to see William, John, and Jack, I assumed they were already climbing down. Jack must have led them to it.

When Father drew his cloak over his nose, I did the same, but smoke choked my nostrils and stung my eyes. Fire danced around us, tongues of orange and red licking at the sky. Sweat drenched my face, even in the freezing air.

"You can't escape me," it roared.

I gasped. A monster with a voice seemed unnatural, more so than the monster itself—an abomination straight from Hell.

"Jaclyn, cover yourself with your cloak and run through the fire. I'll hold him still." Father pushed me back and waved his sword in front. "Jaclyn. Hurry."

"No. I will not leave you. You come with me."

"If we both go, he'll catch us. Go, Jaclyn, before the fire worsens."

I held my dagger in front of me, swinging in rage, wishing I was strong like the monsters or had magical powers like a witch. If monsters could be real, why not magic?

The other monsters seemed afraid of the fire, as they backed

135

away and dared not enter the blistering circle. But Longinus did not fear it.

Then I remembered the dagger cutting me open. I should have bled to death, but I hadn't. Nor would I burn from the fire, I was sure of it.

Just as I stepped forward to lunge at Longinus, arms circled my waist, yanking me through the flames.

Chapter Seventeen
The Beanstalk

ire engulfed me. I was consumed by pain and heat, as though my every bone and muscle had melted. But shortly after, I found relief when the frigid air washed over me.

"Jack." I screamed from the top of my lungs when he came through the flames. "I'm going to kill you. I swear it."

"You're welcome." He looked at me as if I should be thankful, patting out the fire that had caught his cloak and mine. "I'm sorry but I couldn't find your father when I went back. He might have run back into the cave."

I gave him an angry stare and searched for my father through the flames. "Father! Father!"

The fire prevented me from seeing him, and Father did not answer. I ran from one end to the other, frantically searching for a way in. The flames reached higher than before, causing me to lose my courage to run through. I also didn't know how much it had spread.

My eyes burned, and I coughed in the smoke. I hollered deep within my throat so Father could hear. "I promise. I'll find a way to save you."

I reached out as if I could touch. My heart, my heart, oh my heart. It dropped out of my chest, into the fire.

Please, be safe Father. May angels watch over you.

Jack gripped my shoulders. "We shall save him, but we need help."

Anger scorched through my veins. How dare Jack take me away from my father? How dare he make such a decision for me?

"No one will help us. Not even your brothers are here to save their own father." I threw up my arms.

He looked down in shame and then met my gaze. "We need to go and warn the town. We are their only chance."

"We? Where's your father and John? Did they not—"

"My father and John are safe. They went down first. I stayed behind for you and your father."

I glared at him, but I felt thankful he cared. "You go, and I shall stay."

Jack did not have a chance to answer. A lit torch flew high above us and landed close to the beanstalk. I assumed by Longinus's doing. Any second, the beanstalk would catch fire.

A rope was suddenly around my waist. I turned to Jack, who tied the other end of the rope around himself. He grabbed me before I had a chance to stop him, and my stomach lurched into my chest as I leapt to a giant leaf. Then I slid down the beanstalk at ferocious speed, Jack ahead of me.

"Jack." My arms went around his neck, and I shifted onto his back.

"Hold on tight and don't let go!"

He held onto the stalk with one hand, his dagger with the other, cutting through stems as we plummeted from leaf to leaf.

He must have planned this before he'd pulled me out of the fire, and I had been too busy to notice.

Having no choice, I held on to him, and I, too, helped chop the stems with my dagger, but I didn't have to work hard. William and John had already cut many of them, as they were much farther down.

Bright red flames covered the top of the beanstalk, following us and filling the air with smoke. My heart shattered, and dark despair gripped my soul. Father remained with the monsters.

I clutched my chest from the torment, my breath stolen from me. *Oh, Father. My poor father. I'm so sorry.*

I would go back for him. I'd promised with my life. Jack was right. We needed more men. And we had to convince the rest of the town to fight or run.

"Jack, hurry!"

"I'm trying."

His muscles flexed and worked as fast as his arm allowed. My aching arms shook. I had no energy left. The scorching flames spread faster, and the sky looked like it was on fire, as if God blew angry breath upon us. It would have been beautiful had it not been so dangerous.

We plunged at incredible speed. My stomach flew to my chest, and I lost control of my muscles. My body collided with the broad, flat leaves as Jack and I tangled and twisted together. Falling never seemed to end.

Luckily, as we neared the bottom, a thicker growth of leaves cushioned our fall, and we did not crash as hard as we should have. Unfortunately, though, I had lost my dagger.

I cursed, and something caved inside me, as though I had lost a limb, or perhaps a piece of Father. And to make matters worse, I landed on top of Jack with an unladylike grunt.

Jack groaned.

Sorry, Jack. But you deserved it. But thank heavens I landed with no broken bones.

I sucked in air and then panted with relief. Jack lay still as his breath mixed with mine.

We were face to face until I pushed up to keep from crushing him, but I could move no farther. I hadn't forgotten about the rope. His smirk let me know he was thinking something naughty.

"You don't want a kiss, but would rather lie with me instead?"

Even though he jested, he winced when he laughed. It sort of made me smile. I tried to move, but he held on to my arms.

"Let me go. I'm still mad at you."

"You know the reason I took you, do you not? I promised."

"You almost killed me. Such madness to fall down the beanstalk."

"Aye, but I didn't kill you. I knew what I was doing."

"My father," I said with such wretched sorrow in my heart, holding back tears.

Jack winced, and I saw sadness in his eyes too.

"I promise with my life, we'll save your father as soon as we gather help." His expression changed to a playful one. "Now, if you would stop making eyes at me, we could get going."

A small guttural sound escaped me and I scowled at him.

But he merely waggled his eyebrows.

Oh, he was so arrogant, so supremely sure of himself.

I planted my hand on the rope, ready to untie us, when he wrapped his arms around me, rolled on top of me, and pinned my wrists down. His stunning green eyes pierced me, reaching to the depth of my soul, and lingered.

"Oops. Sorry." His tone was soft, eyes on mine.

I pinched my eyebrows together. "How did you know to bring a rope?" It was an odd question, but I wanted to know.

He shrugged. "I always have a rope around. I never know when I'll have to tie someone up." Giving me a crooked smile, he winked.

I glared at him.

"Unfortunately"—he peered up—"I must end this tryst. We're about to be crushed by fried beans."

For a second, I'd forgotten the beanstalk was on fire. Jack's presence made me absent-minded. We had fallen so fast we'd left behind the fire. Though the fast drop had put distance between us and the blaze, it had followed us down.

He got up halfway and pulled me up at the same time. I would have resisted, but getting squashed under burning beans did not appeal to me. Giant, burnt leaves drifted down on the breeze. Worse still, lightning struck and thunder exploded almost immediately after the rain began to fall.

A drop splashed on my nose and then a couple more, a little bit faster. The beanstalk leaves gave us shelter, so we did not feel the rain much. I hoped it would put out the fire.

Then I recalled I had two more beans in my boot.

"Jack. Jaclyn." William approached us, followed by John leading two horses, one of them Angel. He looked relieved to find us, but then he looked beyond me. "Where's your father?"

"We got separated by the fire…" Violent shudders shook me and words stuck in my throat.

Jack blinked as water washed his face, and finished for me. "Richard held Longinus back so Jaclyn could escape. We need to gather as many men as possible and go back for him. We don't have much time. The monsters will be coming after us, and then they will head to the town. Longinus is set on revenge. He wants human blood."

"We must think on it. I'm with you on going back to save Richard. But you're right, son, Longinus wants revenge. We don't have much time."

William tilted his head back, and I followed his line of vision. The rain had subdued the beanstalk fire somewhat, and cleared away most of the smoke. But the look on William's face said it all. Hell had come to our land.

I gasped and held my breath at the most frightening sight I'd ever seen—monsters swarmed down the mountain like ants from a disturbed anthill. Their long nails dug and scratched as they made their way down, like cats sliding down a curtain. I recalled the deep grooves in the bare rock and shivered.

"We need to go." Jack turned to me, rain dripping from his hair. He reached behind me to raise the hood of my cloak, and did the same to his.

"Thank you." I shivered. The hood did little to protect me from the freezing rain soaking through, but it would have to do.

I ran to Angel and nuzzled her, my cheek against her neck. It was so good to see her alive and well. I had worried about her.

"Jack, you ride with Jaclyn on her horse, and I'll ride with John

142

on yours." William adjusted his hat and cloak. "Hurry. Let us not waste another second. We must reach the village first." He placed the palm of his hand up as if to catch the rain. "It's falling faster, a good sign. It will slow the monsters too."

William and John mounted Jack's horse and took off. Angel, on the other hand, resisted Jack. Every time he tried to get a foot into the stirrup, she stamped and moved to the side. Finally, after a bit of Jack coaxing and whispering sweet nothings in her ear, she surrendered.

"Go, Angel." I gave her soft rubs. "If he becomes too much of a burden, feel free to kick him off."

Jack's snort brushed the back of my neck, sending pleasant tingles down my spine. The faster I rode to town and gathered the men, the faster I would rescue Father. When arms sneaked around my waist, I slapped them.

"Keep your hands to yourself."

"I need to hold on to something. What if I fall?"

"Fine." I sighed.

The wind stayed with me, as I rode hard into the dark forest. The cold wrapped around me, but Jack's hold gave me comfort. I welcomed his warmth, and his body sheltered my back from the rain, but it also bathed me in a pleasant tingling sensation.

My mind was upon him, for his chest pressed against my back and his thighs rubbed mine with every stride. I liked the feeling, too much. Though his advances unnerved me, Jack was being a good friend, and I appreciated his help.

He had promised to go back with me to help Father, and I believed him. He might be arrogant and stupid at times, but he

143

was also a man of honor and integrity. He could have left me by the fire, but he had not.

"She's just as stubborn as you," Jack said. "You make a perfect team."

"You better watch what you say. Angel might kick you off."

Jack's hands crept higher, so I slapped them lower.

"Sorry, just slipped. We are bouncing to Angel's stride, after all."

He snickered in my ear, and though I could not see his expression, I knew he wore a smirk.

"Jack." William's concerned voice bellowed in the darkness.

"Behind you, Father."

When I glanced over my shoulder, the beanstalk darkened and disappeared. The fire had swallowed it up, leaving no trace. But the mountain remained black as night.

The mountain played tricks on my eyes, swaying like tree limbs in the breeze under the weight of the monsters climbing down. And the sight alone paralyzed me.

Angel felt my desperation and fear. She galloped over the muddy ground fast as lightning. The darkness and the rain would not slow her down, for Angel could reach home even with her eyes closed. I trusted her, as she did me.

Angel caught up to Jack's horse and galloped by its side. Two bright lanterns, like two north stars, led the way out of the forest. When the road split into two, we took the one I'd not traveled before, toward Jack's town.

Chapter Eighteen
Jack's Town

When I opened my eyes, fleecy clouds stretched across the periwinkle sky, a start of a new day. My head rested on Jack's shoulder. While one of his arms held me, the other one held fast to the reins, guiding Angel onto an unfamiliar road.

Blood rushed to my cheeks, despite the bitter wind. I sat up and wiped drool off my chin, ashamed to have fallen asleep. My damp tunic clung wetly to my skin, and strands of hair stuck to my face. But I need not worry about such foolish things. I could bear embarrassment, but I could not bear the thought of Father imprisoned on the mountain with the monsters.

When we passed the barren winter fields, we came upon barns and cottages. At last we reached the village and the pungent scent of soil and dung welcomed me.

"Sorry," I said. "I closed my eyes and fell asleep."

"You need not be sorry. 'Tis good you rested."

My cheeks flushed, but I did not respond.

I had been so busy fighting for my life I had not given much thought to learning my parents were not truly my own. Who had been my real mother and father? Were they living? Why had they left me? What was the purpose of the lance?

Perhaps my real mother had had me out of wedlock, and she'd given me away to escape the shame. I made up stories. I was good at that. Many questions plagued me, but only the woman who gave me life could answer them.

As for me, the people who had raised me were my truest mother and father. They had given me food, shelter, love, and all I needed. After we rescued Father, we would have the chance to talk. And if by a miracle chance of fate my real mother found me, it would not change my love for Mother and Father.

But how different might my life be? Would I live in a town? A castle? Did my mother have Mary's blood?

I frowned, tightened my fists, and cursed at fate, for I knew these questions would never be answered. And worse still, my life had been a lie, and the truth finally revealed itself.

Jack slowed Angel when children greeted us with smiles and laughs. Their faces and clothes bore smudges from tumbling about the dirt and grass. I took in the unexpected beauty of his town. The houses sat on parsley-green pastures surrounded by lazy hills, unlike the tight spacing of homes in other towns.

Some of the homes were covered with living grass, making it seem like they were part of the landscape. Behind the hills, a blue and silver waterfall splashed into a stream where women washed clothes. The sheep, cows, chickens, geese, and other animals roamed within pens at each house we passed. The welcoming atmosphere made me feel at home.

Men, women, and children came out of their houses and gathered about with curious eyes. Some stared in confusion, but most smiled broadly. I smiled back and wished I'd had neighbors and such kinship growing up. Though I understood why my parents felt the need to keep me away from others and how much they had sacrificed for me, but I still missed it.

We stopped at John's house to deliver him, and then we traveled several houses down. Two men charged out when we dismounted. Their similarly dark hair, features, and build proclaimed them to be Jack's brothers.

"Father. Jack." The first brother's voice burst to life.

"James. Jonathas."

William offered the biggest smile I'd ever seen him give, and welcomed James into his arms, and then the second brother.

The brothers embraced Jack, patting each other on the back. I recognized James as the oldest, and the love between them warmed my heart.

Where was their mother? I waited patiently to ask after they exchanged news.

"We're sorry. They would not let anyone leave," Jonathas explained.

William frowned. "Who would not let you?"

"Father Henry," James answered. "He declared God told him we should not face the devil, and God would save us. He also said God told him the whole village would be sent to Hell if they sought the devil. We tried leaving, but every time we did, men stopped us with whatever weapons they had. Please, Father, believe me. We tried."

William nodded, patting James's back. "I believe you, and I know exactly what men you speak of."

"How did you get out, Jack?" Jonathas scratched his head.

147

"I ran when the meeting began. When Father is absent, you two represent the family. But they would not miss me."

Silence.

I flinched when the brothers turned to me.

"Is that—?" Jonathas's eyes roamed my body, especially my face.

He studied me so closely it made me nervous. Then he tugged at my tunic and put a hand on my hair. James, the eldest, gave me a knowing smile. He recognized the grown-up me.

I thought I heard a light growl from Jack, who stood beside me.

"Yes, 'tis Jaclyn. You remember Richard's daughter?" Jack stood taller, crossing his arms. Almost predatorily.

Hearing my father's name thrusted a dagger into my heart. Thoughts of my parents drove me to the edge of despair. There was much to fear.

Tired, hungry, weary of horror and assaulted by Longinus—the nightmare had just begun. Monsters threatened to wipe out entire towns, and they were on their way. When would they reach this place?

Today? Tonight? Tomorrow? No one was safe.

Though I tried to be as polite and cheerful as Jack's brothers, my somber thoughts distracted me. I wanted to crawl into my chamber and cry or vomit. Beaten like a rug and tempted to lose faith, I prepared my heart for the dread to come.

Where was God? Would He stop Longinus from ripping out God's people's hearts and damning their souls? How could I remain strong and not lose hope when darkness clouded my faith?

Why was this happening to us?

Why?

"Indeed I do remember you, Jaclyn." James went around Jack and picked me up. "You've grown to a beautiful lady. I wish we had met in happier times."

Jonathas pushed James to the side and held me tightly. "Little Jaclyn, the one Jack had fancied. I believe under those rags and dirt, you've become quite beautiful."

Despite my worry, I blushed, ignoring the jest about Jack having a crush on me. Their teasing almost distracted me from the grim fate that might await my father and the village.

"I did not fancy Jaclyn, you dolt." Jack smacked his brother on the head.

Then Jonathas wrestled Jack to the ground.

"Boys. There's no time to waste on tomfoolery." William cleared his throat and flashed a glance at me, seemingly embarrassed by his sons' actions. "We need to gather men tonight to rescue Richard, and no priest's men will stop us. We must also warn the people. Monsters are coming."

That got their attention, and they stiffened.

"What monsters, Father? They're coming here?" Jonathas looked around as though one breathed on his neck.

"Have you gone mad?" James asked.

"Let's get in the house and I'll explain." William tilted his head. "First, we need to feed ourselves. James, take the horses to the stable, clean them up, and fetch them water and food."

I followed William into the house. The fire crackling and the scent of something delicious cooking in the pot churned my stomach. Jack's house looked like mine, even the barn. Inside, the house was tidy with simple furniture and an extra bedchamber, but I still saw no sign of their mother.

I recalled Jack's mother being pretty and a bit plump. She had been kind and gentle the few times I had seen her.

"Please sit." Jack's eyes followed me like a hawk's. He guided me to my place across from William and sat next to me.

Jonathas placed three bowls of soup on the table. Keeping his gaze on me, he said, "We had our fill before you arrived. Please, eat."

The vegetable and barley soup felt like heaven's touch to my belly. I felt guilty eating a warm meal when Father suffered in the hands of the devils. I took another sip, savoring the delicious taste, reminding myself I needed the strength. Father would want me to eat.

I cleared my throat. "Jonathas, has my mother gone?"

Mother had traveled alone at night to William's town. I hoped and prayed she was well. My throat tightened, and I held my breath for his answer.

"Yes." Jonathas sat beside his father. "We are thankful for her journey here. Days or weeks might have passed before we thought to worry. We are also grateful for you. If not for you, none of us would have known the monsters took Father."

William nodded solemnly and slurped his soup.

I lowered my head, thinking about Father.

Jonathas's forehead creased with worry. "After the meeting, when no man volunteered for the search party, she said she needed to go home to you. We sent Luke, a helper from the church, so she would not ride alone. Did you not see her? Wait. How did you…?" He scratched the back of his head.

I hadn't told Jack's brother I had been with them in the cave. They must think I had come in search of Mother.

A gust of wind blew inside the house when James entered. He headed for the fire and rubbed his arms briskly as his teeth chattered.

James blew into his cupped hands, shivering. "It's freezing out there. It seems colder than yesterday."

"I found Jaclyn at Black Mountain." Jack cut a glance at me and rubbed the back of his head nervously. "She went alone." There was a surprise admiration in his tone.

I forgave him for taking me away from my father until he opened his mouth again. "Jaclyn, you could have been killed."

His tone was mild, but I disliked being scolded by Jack in front of his brothers like a child. Father had trained me to use a sword and raised me to be strong, to defend myself. Had he not seen my strange healing power? Had he not heard Longinus's words?

After everything we had seen and survived, maybe Jack believed it all madness. Longinus's claims were outlandish. Perhaps *I* was going mad.

The brothers' eyes grew wider as if waiting for me to say something, but I kept silent. I pressed my lips together and dug my nails into my palms underneath the table. As a guest in Jack's home, I would respect him and his family and keep calm.

People judge parents by their children's manners in public. I would make my parents proud. But then again, our circumstances were not normal, and I wasn't with strangers. Our parents were old

151

friends, so I decided to speak up after all.

"What's wrong, Jack? Awed by my skill in battle? After all, I did knock you down a couple of times."

I got up to take my bowl to the wash basin, hiding the heat rising up my neck. Sure, I had bested Jack, but belittling him in front of his brothers made me no better."

The brothers chuckled.

"I like her," James said, eyebrows waggling. "She has wit and fire."

"She is strong." Jonathas ruffled Jack's hair.

"Be silent." Jack scowled and swatted his brother's hand with his spoon. "She's special. She's—"

I understood he felt deeply worried for me, but I didn't want Jack to spill who I was. I spun around and shook my head, begging Jack not to say more about what had happened. Healing as I did was a mystery, the others would think it the devil's work.

William's chair slid back and he rose.

I welcomed the interruption.

"I'll be in the barn to gather a few things." William headed for the door. "James and Jonathas, come with me. I'll explain about the monsters, and then I need you to get the town ready for the meeting. We can't wait for nightfall. That is when the monsters will come for us. We must get the people out before sunset."

William had seemed to be deep in thought throughout the dinner conversation. I was glad he had not heard our childish nonsense.

Jonathas fixed his hat and stopped when he met my eyes. "What will Jaclyn do? Women are not welcome at the meeting."

152

"Some men don't deserve to be at the meeting. They are not men. They are cowards. I've seen braver women." Jack looked my way.

"I agree with you, brother. But the law is the law. However"—James adjusted his cloak and glanced at my body—"she's already dressed like a man. Pull back the hair, have the hood cover most of Jaclyn's eyes, keep the dirt on her face, and they will not know." He winked.

Dirt on my face? Dear heavens.

I hid my face, embarrassed.

Jack came toward me with his and his father's bowls in hand. "I'm sorry." He set the spoons inside the basin. "'Twas not my intention to scold you like a child."

"I forgive you." I gazed at the glistening fire, unable to meet his eyes. "We've been in Hell the past couple of days. I'm sure you're not yourself."

I leaned against the wall for support and studied him as he tossed more wood into the fire. His perfect chestnut hair fell over his brow. Thick eyebrows and long eyelashes, too beautiful for a man, framed his stunning green eyes. He had high cheekbones like his mother and a strong jaw like his father. And the stubble along his jawline made him very appealing.

"Where is your mother? I have not seen her yet." I asked the question I'd been puzzling over.

Jack lowered his head but then met my gaze—his face a mask of serenity. "My mother passed a year ago."

Pain and pity scorched my heart, and words failed me. "I'm sorry, Jack."

I draped my arms around him and my head rested against the wall of his hard chest. He smelled like wood and burnt leaves, and my heart thundered.

He was so strong, yet so gentle. His body firm, yet so comforting. He tightened his arms around me.

"Jaclyn."

His breath brushed my flesh, like the whisper of a warm breeze.

My head spun as he nestled his cheek next to mine. The roughness of his stubble prickled my skin, but oh so pleasantly. Then his lips moved and stayed at the corner of mine as if asking for permission to continue. His mouth, hot and persuasive, sent temptation trembling throughout my body.

Not here. Not now.

It felt wrong to enjoy being held when Father's life dangled in a monster's hands, and every town nearby would suffer. Closing my eyes, I gently pushed him away. I felt a rush of regret when he gave a disappointed sigh.

Jack turned to the table. "My mother died from a high fever that would not break."

"I'm sorry," I said again. I reached out a hand to him, but dropped it. "I don't remember much about your mother, but the few times I saw her, she was nice to me. She was kind and beautiful."

He probably did not care about my opinion, but I wanted to let him know what I thought of his mother.

Jack sauntered inside one of the chambers and returned with a small rag in his hand and a long crimson fabric. "They were hard times after she passed. We never knew how much Mother did for

154

us until we had to take on all of her work." He lifted the rag and lightly scrubbed my face.

I stilled, surprised by his kindness, but I took his wrist to stop him. "I must look like a man. Perhaps I should keep the dirt."

Jack's lips twitched, his green eyes shining. "You're too beautiful to pass for a man, dirty face or not." Then he stroked along my cheek and my chin.

I flinched and sucked in air. His words touched my heart the way they should not. However, the smooth, heartbreaker Jack I'd known years before might have changed. Perhaps like me, he had grown up. He seemed responsible and more like a man than a boy.

When I pushed his hand away from my face, I saw red lines. "You've cut your hand?" Small cuts crossed his palm. "You must use a salve of willow's bark and honey to help to heal and ease the pain."

"Aye. We have plenty. Four men live here, remember? You care." His eyes glowed again, his grin—wicked, but gorgeous.

He untied my cloak, letting it drop, and then he wrapped the crimson fabric around my shoulder.

I pulled back from his near embrace. "What are you doing?"

"Putting a fresh cloak on you. It's a gift."

I took another step back and the basin brushed against my back. "I can't accept a gift."

"You can return it if you do not want it later, but your cloak is stained with blood."

My own blood.

Jack cleared his throat. "It belonged to my mother and I would be honored if you wore it. I promise it will keep you warm on our

155

journey back to save your father."

The mention of my father brought back our last moments together and the well of my emotions swelled until they nearly choked me. Thought after thought raced through my head. My father. My mother. Longinus. Monsters. How touching Jack's gift was. Jack. *Jack.*

"Shhh. It will be well. We will save your father."

His whispered words calmed me. I closed my eyes, drinking in the moment of safety and warmth with gratefulness. When Jack finished tying the cloak on me, I opened my eyes and smiled.

Jack's cheeks flushed and he grinned.

A screeching wind slammed the door open.

Jack and I jumped apart.

William entered with swords in hands and two daggers secured to his waist and boots. Catching our eyes, he said, "'Tis time."

Chapter Nineteen
Miracle or Work of Evil

When William, Jack, and I entered inside the church, the people sitting toward the back stared at us. I ducked my head lower and clutched my cloak tightly in front of my body. Though the hood over my head covered most of my face, I worried they would know I was a girl.

The men continued to watch me walk cautiously over the stone floor to the front. Then William snaked to the side, away from people's view. I trailed behind him.

Men filled most pews, shoulder to shoulder. A metal cross and a Bible sat on the altar. Candles burned on the tables—flames ascending—gave the feeling of unity and wholesomeness. Light shone through the high windows, giving the room a Heavenly glow.

I felt as though I'd stepped into God's home, though I had no idea what Heaven looked like. Peace flowed through my soul.

"The monsters will not leave their mountain. God will protect us." Standing behind the altar, Father Henry raised his hands. He hadn't seen us come in because he was gazing heavenward, and his loud voice overpowered the sounds of our entry.

James moved in front of the assembled crowd. "If you do not leave your homes today, your family will perish at the hands of the devil."

The crowd roared with criticisms.

"You do not know what you're talking about, boy," one hollered.

"Have you seen the monsters with your own eyes?" another asked.

"I will not leave the home I've built," someone said from the back of the room.

Jonathas stood beside his brother and raised his hand to quiet everyone. "I understand how you feel. Truly I do. Our home is here as well. But my father has seen the monsters and so has Jack. They tell us the monsters are coming. They will come for you and your family. So run, I say."

"How do you know they'll attack our town? Why would they come here and not another?" one asked from the right. "If you say your father has seen a monster, then let him speak. Where is your father?"

"Right here." William raised his hand, walking faster to the front.

Jack and I followed him forward, but stopped next to his brothers.

"What my son says is true. They're on their way here and to every town."

"How do you know this?" a man asked.

William lifted his brow, and his fingers gathered into a fist. "Did you not know of my capture? Where do you think I've been the past few days? Not just me, but the other men. Our own Aldwin and Peter were killed by the very monsters my son spoke

158

of."

Gasps and muttering filled the room.

"How did you survive?" one asked.

"I do not know why the monsters did not kill me, but took me instead, along with John and Richard. The master of the monsters, named Longinus, warned us he would kill everyone."

"I'm to believe he let you go to warn us? A talking monster with a name?" The stranger burst into a chuckle, holding his belly. "Now that's a tale to tell."

Laughter rang loudly around us.

"You stupid fools," William snarled, his nostrils flaring. "Don't you recall the reason we moved away from the Black Mountain sixteen years ago? I led you away from these monsters."

"No man ever saw these monsters then. How are we to know they will come out now?" a young man asked.

"You must believe me. My son Jack saved us, but he could not reach Richard. Demon fire surrounded him, and he is still in the monsters' hands. We must help."

William did not say my name. His people would think him crazy if he did.

"You don't need to go back. Let the monsters burn in the flames of Hell." Father Henry gripped the altar and wiped the sweat beading on his forehead. "God has spoken to me. Kneel before the Lord and pray. He will protect all those who believe and those who mind their own business and stay put."

"What is to be of Richard, then?" Jonathas asked.

The room went still. You could have heard a pin drop.

"Does Richard not have a son?" a man questioned.

159

"Let his own son save him," another added before the question had been answered.

"He has a daughter. She would be of no use."

"Let his daughter save him." A man made a funny sound, as if he'd pressed his lips together and blown.

I scowled. It took every ounce of my will not to punch his face.

Jack's shoulders rose, and his body shook. I tapped his arm to calm him. He might speak in my defense, and it wasn't worth the risk of revealing myself a girl in their presence. Jack's family might get ridiculed or kicked out.

"Richard is not of our town. We have no obligation to save him. He is only one person," one said angrily from the back right.

"Yes, we do." John stepped out from the second pew. "Richard fought for our king alongside many of us. Not only is he an honorable man, but he also helped build our town. He might not have set his roots here, but many of your houses were made with his sweat and blood. And he helped us when he had his own family to take care of, so do not tell me he's not one of ours."

I had never been told Father helped so many, so selflessly, and I had been too small to remember. Father had done so many worthy things, but not once had he bragged about them.

"He forced us to move," a man said from the first pew. "He spoke of monsters then, but they never came. We moved and started over for no reason at all. Leave him to his monsters."

"Aye," a group of them agreed.

Many of them clearly bore a grudge about the move; one by one, a chant of assent resounded around the church.

"Nay, he's our friend. Many of you know him." A man stepped

160

in to the middle of the aisle to make his voice heard.

His gray hair contradicted the strength of his voice.

"He's loaned you silver and goods and never asked for anything in return. He gave you food and shelter when you had none. What kind of man gives away his coin and labor to others?" He pointed to a bearded man. "Would you?" Then he turned the other way and pointed at another man. "Would you?" And then he asked the same to countless men, who turned away their faces. When they could not reply, he said, "I thought not. We are all sinners. But a man like Richard, who helps strangers, should be treasured. We should all learn from him. He is worth saving."

Then chaos erupted.

"Stop." William whistled. "We're wasting time. I need men to rescue Richard, and those who are afraid may stay. It will be a dangerous battle. For those of you with families, I suggest you start heading toward the hill and hide. Go now."

"I will come with you, William."

"I will go."

"As shall I."

A group of men, along with the old man whose speech about my father had brought tears to my eyes, raised their hands. I thanked them silently for their bravery.

"Men, ride with me." William paced down the aisle and I followed him.

"Stop." Father Henry raised his voice. "No one leaves. I command you in God's name to stay and pray. The hands of the Lord will protect us. The monsters will not come. God will send the devils back to Hell." He opened the Bible and read the scriptures aloud. "'I am Alpha and Omega, the first and the last ... I am he that liveth, and was dead; and, behold, I am alive for evermore...'"

I'd thought Father Henry was a little *not right* in his mind, and this only confirmed he had gone mad or senile.

Some of his trusted followers—big, strapping men—blocked the door.

Fools. They were all fools.

I had pictured it differently. The men would respect William and the good name of my father. Families would gather their belongings, as much as they could, and leave for the hills. Those men who had no families would come with us to help rescue Father. None of that was happening, all because of Father Henry. The church had a lot of power, but I did not think it would make men quietly await their deaths.

"We have every right to leave. You can't keep us prisoners," Jack said, the first time he'd spoken since we had arrived.

"You go when Father Henry says you go." One of the guards stepped closer to Jack.

The other men stood in front of the door and narrowed their eyes, looking like they could eat Jack for a meal, though Jack was strong in his own right. The men glowered when Jack and his brothers pulled out their daggers.

Jack jabbed his dagger in the air to push back the guards. "I'll cut your throat, giant. Now let us out."

William pushed Jack out of the way. "No, son. You will not spill blood in the church." He turned to Father Henry, who was still praying. "Father Henry, I demand you let us go, or

162

unnecessary blood will shed among these people tonight."

Some of the men gathered around Father Henry and the voices of prayer carried louder than before. The men in the church chose sides, as if for a battle, and appeared to be evenly matched.

Every moment wasted trying to convince Father Henry shortened the chance of Father's rescue. It also allowed the monsters to get closer. The monsters could be tearing through the town nearest Black Mountain right then. I refused to stand still.

My stubbornness might kill me one day.

I ran to Father Henry, my heart thumping. When I reached him, I pulled a dagger from my boot with my trembling hand, rolled up my sleeve, and held it just above my arm. He looked terrified and backed away, so I had no time to think.

"This monster who calls himself Longinus is cursed by God." I kept my voice deep, trying to sound like a man. "He wants revenge and will take it from innocent people. Good and evil are at war, and we are in the middle of it. Here is your proof."

I sliced open my arm and held it above my head. Crimson liquid ran down like the blood of the lamb. I turned slowly so they could see the cut heal right before their eyes. Loud gasps pounded in my ears.

"A monster," someone shouted.

Someone from behind me pulled down my hood.

The room hummed.

"She's a girl."

"She's a witch."

"Damn her to Hell."

"Blasphemy."

"Kill her."

What have I done?

Now that I had acted, the decision seemed to be made in haste.

People fear what cannot be explained. And I was something that should not exist, could not be understood. Miracles could happen. People prayed for them all the time, but when a miracle appeared before them unasked, they called it a work of evil.

Believing in God's miracles was one thing, but seeing one with your own eyes was another. Only the true believers would embrace someone like me.

Jack ran for me, pushing through the sea of men coming toward me. I should have moved, done something, at least run, but somebody held me from behind.

Something shiny sparkled for a second in the sunlight. Someone crashed into me from the side and knocked me down before the sword could strike.

"Jack." I recognized the scent of him, like the smell of the forest after the rain.

Jack yanked me up. "Next time, give me some warning." Releasing me, he turned to punch a man in the face.

"Duck." I socked a man poised to take a swing at Jack from behind.

"Thank you." Jack's eyes rounded in surprise. "You've got quite a punch."

"My father taught me well. Let us leave."

I got a view of the whole church when we climbed over pews to move faster. Men were bloody from punching each other, and bodies tumbled about.

William opened the door with the help of his sons. They had to pommel a few men in doing so. Some men stayed in church while most scrambled out and jumped on their horses.

Good for them. I assumed they would gather their families and run. I prayed they would.

"John." William pulled him to the side. "You need not come. You've been through enough. I need you here. Gather everyone and lead them to the hills. Pair up men and send them to warn other towns. They may not listen, but at least we've done our best."

John embraced William. "Godspeed, my friend. Save Richard."

"You spoke well of Richard. Everything you said is true. Thank you. I could not have spoken half so well. Everyone knew we were like brothers. They would not have believed me."

John nodded. "The reason I had."

William turned to James. "Stay and help John. You are my eldest. People trust you. Take as many as you can and go. Go north. I will find you. Stay safe."

James hugged his father, his brothers, and even me. It broke my heart, not knowing if they would see each other again. I shouldn't have such thoughts and hope for the best instead.

William gave James a shove and hid his sorrow. "Go, my son. Hurry."

"My mother." My words stirred everyone. "She does not know the monsters are coming, and she's home alone."

William gripped my arm just before I was about to get on Angel. "Luke is with her right now, but I did not ask him to stay. I will have some of my men stay with her until this is over."

I clasped his hand in gratitude. "Please, can we stop by to see my mother before we go to Black Mountain? I know it's a little out of the way, but I left home before she came back from your town. She must be worried about me."

William's lips thinned, and his hard eyes bored into mine. Then he examined my cloak. Could he tell it was his wife's? Should I have said something? Surely he realized I wore a different one.

After seconds later, he smiled and answered. "Yes. We will."

My heart felt somewhat at ease. I would have a chance to see Mother. I hoped she'd made it back home safely. She was going to be furious with me, but learning about Father would crush her soul.

"Men, we ride." William settled onto his horse.

"Wait." A man with red hair approached William, eyeing me like a lion stalking a lamb. "This is Richard's daughter?"

"Aye." William guided his horse around to face the man. "Is there a problem?"

"This is no place for her. She'll be killed, or get us killed."

I gasped. My jaw hit my boot. I bit my tongue from spitting rash words.

You dolt. You do not know me.

Father would not approve. No lady of grace and dignity would say such things. Though at times I did not act like a lady, I had a reputation to uphold for my parents' sake.

William watched me as if deep in thought. Why was he taking so long to answer? He'd seen my skill with weapons. Surely he knew I would take care of myself and would not be a burden to them.

My heart raced faster, waiting for his answer. If he'd said no, I would still go, but I would ride behind them without their knowledge. *No!* I would defend myself. I would say something. I had every right. My father's life was at stake, and I would be there to help him.

No man will stop me. No man. Not now. Not ever.

"She is a girl, but I assure you, she is no ordinary girl."

William's words made me smile, and I showed all of my teeth to the red hair man. The man frowned. But I didn't care. He would not make me feel small because I was a woman.

Women have their own bravery. Mother's word encouraged me, gave me strength to assert myself.

William rose from his horse to look over his men. "She rides with us. We have no time to argue. You come with us to battle the evil and save Richard. I do not care if you are a man or woman. We have the devil to fear."

No one else dared argue.

I took off on my horse, leaving John and James behind to bring order to the chaos, while about twenty-five men followed.

"Look." Jonathas pointed to the right to another town as we rode fast alongside the wind pushing us forward.

I shuddered a breath in horror. Smoke shaped like the devil's hand with long fingernails reached for the sky.

It had begun.

Chapter Twenty
Home Sweet Home

y heart leapt. Flames in the distance sent smoke into a gigantic, gloomy blanket over the town. It only meant one thing: the town had been taken by monsters.

I prayed for rain. The swelling, cruel clouds and the freezing temperature all hinted, but none came. Perhaps God had forsaken us after all.

Thoughts of homes destroyed, lives taken, and people screaming and running plagued my mind. And then I remembered Aldwin's and Peter's guts splattered on the ground, their body parts strewn about. It was devastating to imagine the same happening to those people.

I had hoped Longinus's promise to kill every human was empty, but the smoke over a far-away town showed he'd meant it. He wanted revenge. Perhaps he wanted to prove he was better than God.

No … he wanted to be God.

I will be the end of your world and the beginning of a new one when I claim your land. I will be God.

Time was not on our side. The monsters might seek Jack's town next. Hopefully, the people had listened and run as fast as they could, as far as they could. But my heart ached for the burned town.

As if Jack knew I watched him, he twisted his neck to face me with a small smile. That smile let me know he would walk the same path with me every step of the way. At least it gave me some hope we would save Father. Jack had a way of making me feel everything would be well in the end.

The wind favored us, giving us momentum as the breeze moved with us. The cool air brushed against my face and made my cloak flap as if I had wings.

"We'll save your father, I promise." Jack adjusted his rein and patted his horse, as if to let the horse know all would be fine.

He must have seen the worry on my face. I nodded, grateful for his words. Again, I found myself mentally thanking Jack. In my wildest dreams, I would have never thought he would be giving me comfort, strength, and the most important thing of all—hope.

When we were younger, I'd despised Jack. In days gone, I had mistaken Jack's playfulness for meanness and spite. He'd pulled my hair, poked my side, and played tricks, making me scowl while he laughed. How wrong I had been about him.

Little Jaclyn, the one Jack fancied, Jonathas had said. Could it be true?

Heat flushed my cheeks every time I glanced his way, and I scolded myself.

As we rode together, behind the men, I looked at the past with new eyes.

"Did your mother tidy your hair?" Jack touched the long braid down my back with the tip of his finger. His lips twisted up at one

169

side, and his green eyes grew darker.

I yanked my braids away. "Don't touch my hair, you heathen."

"You have no kind words for me? Perhaps you are ashamed because you fancy me?"

My face turned red-hot, and I trembled with anger. "Nay. I do not. You smell like a goat. Where did you get such a witless notion?"

I squeezed my fists by my side, ready to punch his face if he said one more idiotic thing. I looked over my shoulder to where James and Jonathas stood, making sure they could not hear us.

They chatted with other boys by the horses. Our families rarely met since we lived so far away, but once in a blue moon we would gather for a feast.

Jack's eyes grew wider, and then his lips spread into a smirk. "'Tis true. You *do* fancy me, Jacky?"

Jacky? What a stupid name.

Though I'd die before telling him, Jack was handsome, and seeing him made my heart skip. Emotions I didn't understand fluttered through me, but the thought of falling in love with such an arrogant, dumb boy made me ill.

Instead of responding with words, I aimed a fist at his right cheek. But he blocked my punch and spun me around so fast I felt dizzy. Maybe the thought of being in his arms stole my balance.

Jack's chest pressed into my back. Even for a skinny boy, he had strong muscles.

"Next time you try to punch me, Jacky, I will kiss you. Mark my words." Then he let me go.

I narrowed my eyes, and flared my nostrils in annoyance. "Do not call me Jacky, you dolt."

Thoroughly flustered, I cursed at him and walked away. He wanted to kiss me? Just for a second, I wondered what that might feel like.

When I peeked over my shoulder, I saw girls surrounding Jack, talking and giggling, but he paid them no mind. Instead, he kept his eyes on me, and his gaze burned into my soul.

"We're almost there," William announced.

Home.

A familiar road greeted me, and the scent of heather spiraled through my nose, as smoke lingered on the horizon behind. Though the storm clouds had turned and shifted, getting darker, promising rain, excitement and the anticipation of seeing Mother coursed through my blood.

Angel felt the same as I did. Her head bobbed, and her gallop seemed more like a dance.

I thought of different ways to greet Mother and the best way to inform her about Father. Should I charge into the house? Should I wait for her to ask about Father, or just blurt it out?

How should I explain all these men at our doorstep, and how could I let her know I'd found out she was not who had given birth to me?

Please give me strength.

The sun dipped lower, almost gone, and the last rays showed me Mother standing in front of the door as we rode into the yard. Holding a lit lantern, she started toward us. I jumped off Angel and ran to Mother. She embraced me so tightly I feared she would crush me. Her arms reminded me she had always been the only mother I needed.

After releasing me, she scowled. "Where have you been? When I came home, you were gone. I have been so worried about you. I'd thought you chased after your father all on your own." Tears formed in her eyes. "Don't worry me again. We'll talk later. There's so much I want to ask. And you got a new cloak?" She admired it and then she turned to face the men. "Welcome, William and gentlemen." She nodded, greeting them. "Luke has left. There are so many of you. How can I help you?"

William dismounted, dropped the hood of his cloak and approached. "We've come for supper if you have any to spare, and the horses need food and water as well. Then we must be on our way. Do you know Richard is still at Black Mountain?"

Mother gave no answer, nor did her face betray her feelings. "Please, let us be warm. Let me get you some tea. Supper is almost ready, though I hadn't expected so many. It'll be simple, stew and bread, and small portions. And of course, please take care of the horses for your long journey. Come in and please tell me what you know. I've been praying for good news."

When we went inside, Mother attended to the men while I went to my chamber to change my clothes. Dried dirt and mud caked my tunic and breeches. After I changed, I retied my hair. I thought about braiding it, but for some reason, braids reminded me of Jack.

I took off my boots, wiggled my toes, and let the air seep through. Using a rag, I wiped the area of my cheek Jack had tried to clean for me before, and then I wiped between my toes. Afterward, I slid into dry woolen socks, pulled my boots back on, and made sure to feel two beans under my foot. Swinging Jack's mother's cloak back on, I went to join the others.

The men sipped tankards of ale while Mother poured stew into hollowed out, days-old bread loaves. I helped her serve and placed a basket of fresh bread on the table.

"Supper is ready," Mother said. "I've already eaten, so please, go right ahead."

The house seemed even smaller with so many people inside. While most men sat on the floor to enjoy their meal, I stood by the fire to keep warm.

"Sarah, we're on our way to Black Mountain," William said.

Oh God, I dreaded the bad news to come. The carrot I'd just swallowed hadn't been chewed enough. It felt hard and lumpy going down my throat, or maybe that was nerves.

"I am unsure how much Richard has shared about…" He rubbed the back of his head. "As you already know, Richard, John, and I were captured by the monsters, but Richard is still there. He sacrificed his own escape for ours."

Mother busied herself by adding wood to the fire for a few breaths. Then she crumpled to the floor on bended knees.

"Mother." I reached for her, but William got to her first.

William helped her up and held her steadily. After assisting her to the chair, he sat by his men. Then he asked a few men to get the horses ready.

"No," she murmured under her breath. "How is this possible? Richard is a good man. He helps others. Why would God not save my husband?" She paused, covering her mouth. Her lips trembled, and the line on her forehead deepened with concern. "When I saw you, William, I knew you had come with bad news, because why would you be here and not my husband? I hoped to be wrong. I hoped to hear you say Richard"—Mother's lips quivered, and she took a moment to collect herself—"was on his way home."

Mother gazed into William's eyes with such sadness. It killed me.

William explained everything to Mother: Their attempt to lure the monsters out and subsequent capture; how Jack and I had rescued them; that Father had no choice because the fire had prevented him from escaping. Then he told her about the beasts invading the towns. The whole time, Mother clenched her knees.

"Five men will stay behind, Sarah," William said. "I trust these men. They will guard you with their lives. I believe you are safe, and the monsters will only attack towns where people live closely together. Try to keep the fire low and the lanterns away from the windows. The less attention you draw, the safer you will be."

Mother looked at me with tears in her eyes, uncertain. "Jaclyn, will you stay?"

I wanted so badly to say yes, but I dipped my chin instead. "I must go. Father needs me."

She did not like my response. More tears fell down her cheeks. She was afraid for her husband and her only child.

"It's too dangerous." Her words came out soft and gentle, like her, like her heart.

I took her hands into mine. "Women have their own bravery. Those were your own words."

"I know. I believe. But ... but ..."

Bravery didn't guarantee I would come back home.

I blinked tears away. "Don't worry. We'll bring Father home. Father did not train me for no reason. You told me before, everyone has a destiny and a story to tell. Do you remember?"

She nodded, sniffing. "Fate will lead you to a path on which you are meant to be."

"This is my destiny. This is my story." I knew this to be my fate in every vein, bone, muscle, and in my soul.

Mother's silence told me she believed in my fate, too. And thinking of Father's tale of how the lance and I had come to his doorstep, I knew I had to take the lance with me.

I had not yet even begun to understand, but the lance and I were one. Visions of Longinus and the monsters appeared when I touched the tip, and fate had set its course.

She wiped away her tears and stroked my hair. The love she carried for me showed through her glassy eyes—strong and unyielding. "May God watch over all of you. Please, stay safe."

"I will." I kissed her cheek.

I could not keep my promise. I had a slim chance of returning. However, I needed to have hope. I'd escaped from the monsters once. I could do it again.

William stood and walked to the door. "We can't waste any more time, Sarah. I'm sorry to bring you bad news and have to run."

Mother pressed her dress down, her fingers working over folds and wrinkles. "It must be done. Please bring my family back home safely, as well as Jack and your men."

"I will do my best." He bowed slightly with his hat to his chest. "Thank you for welcoming us into your home and feeding us supper on such short notice."

"It was my pleasure. It's not enough to make your bellies full, but hopefully it will tide you over until the next meal. I will pray for everyone." Mother crossed her arms. Then, with tears in her eyes, she wrapped her arms around me. "Jaclyn. My Jaclyn. Please be safe and come back to me, and bring Father home. I cannot bear to lose either of you."

"I will, Mother," I said with conviction, but my heart ached.

I didn't know if it would be the last time I would see her. Inhaling her scent of fresh baked bread and stew, I took a moment to memorize the warmth and love of her embrace. I would carry it with me to give me strength and hope.

I turned away, dreading leaving Mother alone. Hopefully she would remain safe. She had to.

"Five men will remain with you." William pointed to them. "You know my son, Jonathas. He will keep watch."

Jonathas raised his hand.

"Thank you," Mother said.

I hugged Mother again, the longest I'd ever hugged her. Then I followed William's men out of the house and mounted Angel. Mother handed me a small lantern, like the one she held. The lantern would come in handy at night.

We would pass a trading town before we reached Black Mountain. I wasn't sure what I would find there, since it was the closest town to the mountain, but I had a feeling it wasn't going to be pleasant.

"Wait. I need to get something from the barn. I shall be back."
I did not give anyone a chance to utter a word of protest. I guided
Angel there. After entering the barn, I dismounted and went to
Daniel.

"Hi there, Daniel. I wish to take something, so I'm going to
come in."

I moved past him to the secret storage place. When I opened
it, the only weapon left was the lance. I had hoped by some miracle
there would be other swords and daggers too. I had already taken
the daggers, but having another weapon would give me an
advantage, especially something longer. Releasing a heavy sigh, I
picked up the lance.

"You and I have things to do," I said to the lance. "I do not
know what that might be, but I have a feeling it's something
glorious. It must be. I was born of Mary Magdalene's blood."

I tried to hide the lance when I got back on Angel, but there
was no disguising it. Nobody gave me a hard time about it except
for Jack, who cocked a brow.

"Really? It's twice your size."

"It is not."

"Would you like me to hold it for you?" He guided his horse
around Angel and examined the lance I'd tied along her length.

"No, thank you. It's not heavy."

"Let's go," William said. He gave Mother one last nod and
kicked his horse forward.

"Be safe." Mother let out a soft whimper and wiped her tears.

I waved to her, smiling through a shattered heart. She must
know half my heart wished to stay with her. I needed to be brave,

to let her know everything would be well.

Breaking down in front of her would crush her heart even more. It took every ounce of my will to keep myself together. I had to be strong.

Biting my lips, I recalled mother's words. I would hold them to my heart as I faced the monsters.

Chapter Twenty-One
Monsters Everywhere

hen the moon shone fullest, round like a wagon's wheel, and the shimmering stars graced us with their presence, the night sky took my breath away. Father used to say the stars were angels' eyes.

During the sweltering summer nights, I would sit on the porch and gaze at the sky. Mother would bring out pie, and I would sing songs. My parents would laugh at the stories I told. For the first time in my life, I turned away from the sky. I saw no beauty there—only pain, grief, and death.

Thick, ominous, clouds followed us, like the devil creeping near. Every part of me screamed not to march forward but I had no choice. I journeyed for what seemed like weeks, but when my legs urged me to stretch and my body begged to retire to my chamber, then I knew we were almost there.

My nightmare had come alive. I needed no lantern to see what waited ahead. The fire still raged in small remnants far and wide, like dragon's breath. The pungent scent of rotten flesh assaulted my nostrils, and the feel of the devil's touch crawled along my skin.

I rode faster.

Angel protested the closer we approached, but I urged her to continue and she eventually gave way. Screams and shouts of agony rode the billowing smoke.

I became like stone. Terrified, I followed Jack into the smoke.

The town I had visited just days past had been razed. Some of the stores had burned to ashes, while some still blazed. The hiss and crackle of fire made it difficult to determine if people needed help.

Carcasses and blood covered the streets, along with shattered plaster, wood, and glass. I skirted the debris, trying to stay away from the fire. The ash-heavy breeze blocked my view.

At times the flames blinded me, burned my eyes, and the fast-rising smoke made breathing difficult. Covering my nose with my cloak helped, but it did not keep me from coughing.

It took some time to get to the other end of the town. I passed the area where the old lady had given me the beans. She clearly had some knowledge of magic. Why wasn't she helping these people?

Screams of horror and death tore through the town, sounding like thunder. I rode faster, but the horror spread out before me. My own cries melted in my throat, and my muscles would not move. Blood stained the ground ... so much blood. Like Aldwin and Peter, their bodies had been ripped to pieces.

Then out from the shadows and smoke, the monsters appeared. Malice-filled amber eyes pierced the night.

I froze, terrorized.

These poor people had no chance. Most held no weapons, and those who did were not skilled in their use; the monsters had killed them easily. They would have been better off running instead of attempting to fight.

Men, women, and children ran like mice, dodging claws and

feet. A monster tore legs from a torso. Another one smashed a body with its feet, and one decapitated another with a simple flick of its wrist.

My stomach twisted and I wanted to vomit. We could stay and fight, but there were too many of them—and I was sure they were in other towns, too.

I gasped in horror. Little children ran and mothers fled with their infants in their arms. Should I stay and help, or try to move past the monsters in one piece? My conscience argued.

William answered my question. "The only way to stop the war is to kill Longinus. Our only two tasks are to bring Richard home and kill Longinus. On our way to Black Mountain, if you must kill a monster, so be it. If we lose each other in the chaos, get yourselves to Black Mountain." William held his sword up in the air. "We ride together."

The men gave a mad war cry as they charged forth behind William. Still devastated by what I had seen, I had no voice left in me. With my dagger in front, I followed.

"Stay close to me. Be careful," Jack said, trying to protect me as usual.

Jack rode swiftly, jumping over burning debris and sometimes circling wreckages, but he always looked behind to make sure I followed as we tried to escape the monsters' attention. When they spotted us, their eyes gleamed with rage. Their roars shook my bones and fear numbed me, and my muscles slacked on Angel's reins. The sound caused me to move slower with unsteady movement.

"Jack. Watch out!"

A monster's claw swooped down at Jack. He ducked and sliced

at the monster's hand with his dagger. The monster shrieked, holding his wounded hand as scarlet liquid dripped down. The monster seemed confused to see us fighting back. The people ran, but not us.

Even with its injury, the monster chased us doggedly. Jack stopped suddenly, almost causing Angel to collide with his horse. The monster loomed above us and I stood right between its legs.

Oh God! Icy chills washed through my bones and I trembled.

Jack cut through its right leg, and having a hunch what he would do, I sliced across the other, just as deep and long. The monster collapsed.

William and his men slashed left and right with their swords as they rode. The men had a pattern of killing the monsters. One would lure its attention, while the others came around and cut through the ankles, legs, or whatever they could reach.

This gave me hope. We might be smaller than them, but we were smarter and faster, and we knew how to work as a team.

I made the mistake by not looking behind me. One lifted me up with its claws. The monster's tight grip choked off my breath, and I wiggled to loosen its fingers.

"Jaclyn!"

Jack must have turned and seen Angel without a rider.

"Jack!"

Jack stopped his horse and grabbed Angel's reins. He pulled her to the side and jumped off his horse and ran to save me. When he reached us, he jabbed his dagger into the monster's toe.

The monster howled, loosened his grip on me, and dropped his arm. I took the opportunity to free both my arms and drove my dagger into the flesh between his thumb and pointer finger. When the monster let me go, I fell. Instead of the ground, I felt arms around me.

"I've got you." Warm breath brushed against my ear.

Jack had caught me. Unbelievable. I embraced him from relief. I had never wanted to feel like a princess who had been saved by the prince, but for a moment, I did.

"Thank you. Next time, it'll be my turn." I scoffed as though it didn't matter. But we had no time to chat. We had monsters to kill and people to save.

I spotted a family hiding behind a burning home in the distance. Everyone was running, but not them. It was the worst place to hide. The house could burn down at any second and leave the family injured, or worse—dead. So I did what any stupid, caring girl would do. I ran toward them.

"Jaclyn!"

Jack's voice rang out behind me. I imagined him rolling his eyes and cursing under his breath. Dodging a monster, I pulled my cloak away from a flaming bundle of debris, while running across a field toward the family.

"Come," I said to the family of four, waving my arms in case they could not hear me.

The father and mother had their arms around young twin daughters. Dirt smudged their faces and nightgowns.

"Jaclyn. We need to go." Jack tried to pull me away.

I yanked my arm back. "Please, let me help this family. I'll go as soon as we get them to a safer hiding place."

Jack did not understand. Once I stopped and got close enough to see their faces, I could not leave them. Their faces would haunt me if I did.

Jack sighed, annoyed, but did as asked like I knew he would. I'd come to believe he would do just about anything for me. When the family did not move, Jack pulled them out and forced them to follow me. I led them away from the fire and around the corner.

"Thank you," the man said, hugging his family. His hands shook, sweat dampened his forehead, and his voice trembled with fear. "I don't understand. Where did they come from? Is this the end? Where is God?"

The man's eyebrows arched, and he raised a hand toward Heaven. I felt sorry for him, and for the town, and every town that would face that monstrous cataclysm. Father Henry had preached often enough about the end of the world. Maybe this was it?

The little hope in me deflated, but then I thought about Father. No, it could not be our end; it would be Longinus's.

Jack patted the man. "'Tis not the end. The monsters will leave soon and move on to another town. Stay here until you know it's safe."

"Aye. Thank you," the man said again.

I'd always thought all men were brave, but I'd come to realize not all men had courage. That man had done his duty by protecting his family. But could he have done what Jack had done? I thought not. Some men were just born to be heroes. Like Father.

After Jack and I got back on our horses, we rode fast toward Black Mountain. Behind us, the diabolical flames continued to spiral up to the endless darkness. My heart broke for the townspeople, and numbing sadness overwhelmed me.

Chapter Twenty-Two
The Beanstalk

By the time we arrived at Black Mountain, dawn had broken, but the sullen clouds prevented light from shining through. I blew out the lantern and rubbed the sleep away. The hope of seeing Father well and alive kept me going forward.

I did not want to think what Longinus might have done to him. Father must be starving and dehydrated. At the thought, I took a water skin out of the saddle and gulped some down.

After Jack's horse and Angel were secure by the stream, so they could drink freely, I untied the lance. William and his men had already tied their horses. They tilted their heads way back to examine the mountain, looking discouraged.

"Father."

William spun to Jack and rubbed the back of his neck. "How do we climb? The other-worldly beanstalk is gone, and the mountain … the mountain." He sighed heavily. "The monster carried me before. How did you get up there?"

"It's going to take us all day," one of William's men said.

Another tilted his head far back. "Holy Mother of God. The mountain is truly black."

"Is there another way up?" someone asked.

185

William's and Jack's foreheads creased, and their lips turned down. They glanced up the mountain, then down, and then up again.

Jack rubbed his chin and stared at the spot from where the beanstalk had sprouted. Had they thought a beanstalk happened to be growing larger than life by chance, perhaps? Even Jack had not asked me about it. Jack must have ridden the beanstalk right under my nose when the plant grew at an impossible speed. That would explain why Jack had been there at the same time as me.

I began to notice William's men staring at me. Perhaps they had in mind I was some kind of abomination, or a miracle. They had seen what I'd done, how my cut had healed itself, but no one had said a word about it. Others looked at me with wide eyes, respectfully. After all, I was just a girl, holding a weapon like a man.

"Where did you get that lance?" one asked.

I stiffened. "It belongs to my father."

I told something of the truth. The lance belonged to me, according to Father's story, but I would not share such words with them.

He backed away and bowed his head. Pointing to the lance, he looked at me with admiration. "I heard a tale about a girl who carried a lance. The tale proclaimed she would destroy evil and bring peace to the land. I never thought to see a woman as brave as you, to have the courage to stand against evil, so I never believed the tale. Now I've seen it with my own eyes, I will follow you and your crusade."

My tongue twisted and could not speak a word. I'd never heard such tale before, and if I had, I would have never believed it to be me. And I didn't now.

How does that explain my ability to heal so fast and the images I see when I touch the tip of the lance?

"I know not of any such tale." I shook my head and slowly put the lance behind my back. This darn thing was too big to hide.

He should not think of me as a savior. It was a lot of pressure, especially when I knew I was going to let him down. I could not kill Longinus. Maybe, collectively, we all could, but I couldn't by myself.

His eyes fell to my arm and gazed intently, as if he could see something there. "But I saw what you did. Blood fell from your wound, and it healed before our eyes."

I shrugged. How could I explain when I did not know what was happening to me?

Jack cleared his throat to bring us back to our purpose. "Ask questions later. Right now, we must figure out how to get up there." Jack narrowed his eyes at me as if I held a secret. "Jaclyn, do you know how to grow the beanstalk?"

I sighed, took off my right boot, shook it until the two beans fell out, and then put my boot back on.

"What are those? Beans?" A man laughed. "A savior with beans?"

I glared at the man who mocked me, and so did Jack. I wanted to introduce him to my fist.

Breathe. Do not give into temptation.

"We don't have time to plant a bean," one said.

"Shut your lips and let her speak." Jack's fists squeezed tightly, and the muscles on his arm hardened as if eager to strike someone.

His shoulders tensed, and his fingers flexed and unflexed.

I picked up the magic beans, dropped one back inside my boot, and held tightly to the other one. Then I prayed. *Please do not fail me. Father needs me.* It had to work.

I tried to recall what had happened or what I'd said before I dropped it, but I had said not a word. And dropping it from halfway up the mountain again to recreate the miracle seemed foolish. I had to have faith. As the image of the old lady came to my mind, I looked at Jack and then everyone else.

With a fist on my waist and my lips curved into a leer, I announced, "Sirs, brace yourselves. Hold on tight."

As I held my breath, I dropped the bean in the same spot where the last beanstalk had sprouted and covered it with dirt. It was the longest couple of seconds of my life.

Please. Please. Please. Don't make me a fool.

Everyone watched the mound of dirt, and they too held their breaths.

Just when I thought I had made a terrible fool of myself, the giant beanstalk burst out right under my feet. Up and up I went. I held on to a leaf while Jack did the same. He gave me a crooked, proud smile, and he held that look all the way up.

A couple of men fell off the beanstalk, and their fading screams died the farther we flew. I felt horrible. They had not grabbed on fast enough. Other men grabbed on to the beanstalk or its leaves with every part of their body, their features terror stricken.

The icy wind brushed my face as I soared, but at the same time, it soothed me. When I peered up, it seemed like I headed for the sky, the clouds readied to swallow me. We shot higher, passing the face of Black Mountain, marred by long, deep claw marks along every inch. I shivered at the thought of how many times the monsters had been in various towns, stealing the sheep and visiting people's homes without them knowing.

Just like before, the beanstalk knew when to stop growing. I stepped onto burnt ground, and the aftermath of the flames stung my nose. Those below me had to climb, so Jack and I extended our arms to help them up.

"What magic is this?" One man clutched his chest.

"I cannot believe it," another man, who had just come up, said and vomited.

"'Tis God's work," another whispered and clapped his hands together to pray.

"Or the work of the devil," someone behind him murmured.

I scowled at his comment. Such a fool. He surely had seen the work of the devil when he'd seen the monsters. I parted my lips to snap at him, but thought better. Father needed me. No need to waste time on petty words.

"This way." Jack waved us directly to the cave.

The men looked hesitant and incredulous as they entered. With swords raised, they cautiously paced forward.

The anticipation of seeing Father made my heart thunder. Every step brought me closer to him, but part of me braced for the worst. Longinus was an evil monster. He had neither heart nor soul, so I would not put it past him to—

I stopped thinking.

Jack held up a hand for everyone to stop. With my back pressed against the wall, I took quiet steps, one at a time. Lanterns and candles surrounded Longinus, who was still in his hideous monster form.

Why hadn't he changed? I knew the answer to my own question. He stayed as a beast so his men could wreak more harm. They changed when he changed. His people were full when he was full; all connected to him.

The monsters had keen hearing, but Longinus ignored us and ate the slab of fresh meat on the table. The table looked too small, as did the plethora of dishes in front of him. Ten monsters skulked on either side of him, as if to protect him. The other countless monsters must be below.

"Welcome." Longinus kept his eyes on his meal. "Do not take me for a fool and think you walk on the wind, you tiny, pathetic people. Lovers of God. Have you come to bow down before me and beg me to remove the monsters from your towns?"

His ears, which had transformed to something akin to a lion's, twitched slightly.

William's men trembled and stared with wide eyes. A few scurried like mice behind Jack and me.

William stepped forward. "No. We've come for our friend. Release him. Tell your monsters to back away, and we can have peace again."

Longinus laughed, not an evil laugh, but a genuine laugh of a person who'd heard a good joke. "Little people have such high demands. You think I will do as you wish? What will it gain me? After all the people are dead, I will be free to live anywhere I please. If there are any survivors, and if they've been lucky enough to live this long, well … I do enjoy eating humans. Your kind forced us out of many places to come to this very mountain. I am only taking back what was mine long before you were born. This world. And as for your friend, you're going to have to go through me." He licked his claws and smoothed his long, ugly tongue along his bottom lip, making a sucking sound. "Perhaps I ate him."

"Liar." I stepped in front of Jack so Longinus could get a clear view of me. It felt so strange to have a conversation with a beast, looking like something between a lion and a human.

His glossy black lips spread wickedly. "Little girl, blood of Mary. Such a harsh word."

I ignored him and moved to the side, ascending a gradual slope toward him. Jack and William followed close on my heels.

Longinus opened his mouth wide to yawn, showing all of his hideous teeth and I squirmed at the sight. His head snapped back to me, and then gazed past me as if he saw something.

"Tell me. How did you climb up here? The beanstalk had burnt down. And how did you manage to grow one so quickly? Who gave you that power?"

His eyes pinned me at his last words. He was not pleased.

"You don't need to know." I gave him the same neutral, but commanding tone back.

"I see. Well, you're just in time to watch your father die."

"Where is he?" I gripped the lance tighter. How I wished to drive it through his heart right now.

Longinus ignored my question and shoved a chunk of uncooked meat into his mouth. Red liquid seeped from the corner of his lips when he tore through with his sharp monstrous teeth. He did not see me as a threat. Even as I approached closer, he did not bother to look my way.

"Where is he?" My shout shook my body. I waved my arms to draw Longinus's attention so William and his men could find Father.

Longinus's deep amber eyes shot to me. His irises pulsed like a heartbeat, glowing and growing darker in rage. "Don't use that kind of tone with me, little girl." The thrumming in his irises stopped and his expression softened. "So, tell me ... do you think your mother would taste as delicious as your father?"

Rage burned through my bones, and my breath escaped sharp and swift. Wrath stole my self-control, and I needed to be in control. Longinus was playing with my mind, so I decided to do the same with his.

"Why don't you tell me what you really did to cause this curse?"

He blinked in confusion, taken aback. I had gotten his attention. With his elbows on the table and a fist resting under his chin, he looked off in the distance.

"No one has ever asked me that, but then again no one has been foolish enough to dare come face to face with me." He sneered and pierced another chunk of meat with his nail. Holding it up as if to examine it, he said, "Like I said before, I was only doing my job, what I'd done to many before Jesus. I did not know who Jesus was. He did not give *me* any sign of divinity. What kind of god would let his own son be tortured?" Longinus shoved the meat in his mouth and set his eyes on me. "I have the answer. The kind of god who does not care."

"You're wrong. You—"

I stopped when Longinus slammed his fist against the table with an echoing bang, knocking food off his plate. The cup tilted. That time, ale spilled and not the blood from the sheep.

"You shall not judge me." He bared his terrifying teeth.

"You knew who He was." My tone rose as loud as his. "But you refused to believe. You turned away."

The lance trembled in my hand. A rush of warmth waved through me, not from a breeze, but something divine. A spirit of truth and revelation wrapped around me, showing me Longinus by the crosses.

"You cared more about what your fellow men thought than you did yourself. You speared Him to prove a point, and so you could save yourself. You even played a game with dice to see who would win his blood-stained robe." I gasped and stumbled back when the words stopped coming, afraid of what I had seen.

"Enough!" Longinus swept an arm across the table, knocking plates and food, and stood.

I flinched, but for Father I continued. "Nay, it is not yet enough. You do not want to hear your fault. You have invented excuses so you can justify what you did. It's not the action, but what you felt in your heart that damned you. You felt nothing when you speared Jesus. You only needed to apologize for being the one who ensured His death. All those who asked for forgiveness were granted it. You just needed to believe. You would have been forgiven, too."

Words flowed out of my mouth, but I did not know from whence they came. I spoke with wit and courage of things I could not know. It was as if I spoke someone else's words.

He froze for a second. "Then tell me, if your god forgives easily, why did He let the curse fall on so many innocents? Mary should have cursed only me, not the gathered crowd. They did no wrong."

"I do not know God's mind. No one does. But why are you taking revenge against my people? They did not curse you. They do not know you. They only know the monsters that have now spilled the blood of many people. Just like you, they have no answers. If you think what has happened to you was unjust, then why are you doing the same?"

Longinus sat back on the ground, his evil amber eyes dancing. After a few long seconds, his lips tugged, and he said, "Because I can."

"Then you are a hypocrite." I marched forward slowly, one careful step after another. "You don't deserve salvation. You deserve the hell you live through every day. Your heart is cold as stone. Mary's punishment for you was righteous. I feel sorry for you no more. I used to. During the nights when you turned, I felt your pain. I heard the screams in my head. I felt everything you felt. I do not know why we are connected, but we are. But fate has brought me to you. As much as I don't want to, I'm here for a reason. I do not know how, but I know I can help you if you let me. You can be free. Your people can be free. Would you not want that for your people, if not for yourself? I see you care about your people. You can help them."

Longinus stood up and took three steps toward me. His long, brown and black fur swayed with each stride. Had I anticipated what he would do next, I would have run, or at least braced myself.

Longinus simply swatted me like I was something in his way.

Chapter Twenty-Three
The Power of the Lance

ain sliced through me as I slammed against the cave wall and fell to the ground, losing my grip on the dagger and lance. I had never known such physical pain, not even when I had fallen off the horse, or hadn't paid attention and received a blow from Father's training sword.

Blood trickled down my chin from a cut lip, and my head throbbed. By miracle, no bones had been broken, I thought, though I would be sorely bruised and aching.

Jack dropped by my side while the other men held up their swords to give me time to come out of my stupor. William and his men came back just in time to help, but without Father.

My heart slammed against the boulder.

Where was Father?

Why had they come back without him? Rage surged through my veins. I wanted to shout. I didn't need their help. I wanted them to find my father. Then I realized they wouldn't have given up easily. They couldn't find him.

"Are you hurt?" Jack helped me up. His eyes roamed my body, assessing if there was any damage.

Though my body slowed by pain, I managed to lift myself half way up. I did not answer. Instead, I asked, "My dagger? My lance?"

Jack glanced to his left and bent to pick up the lance, but he could not. He tried again. Nothing. He tried again. No luck.

"What in heavens?" His eyebrows lifted. "I can't pick it up. What did you do?"

I shrugged, reached down and picked it up effortlessly, and then picked up the dagger. The lance felt so light. Maybe somehow it was magically bound only to me ... and perhaps Father. Father did say the lance and I were at his doorstep. He had to have been able to lift it to hide it. There were so many unanswered questions—the crazy old lady, the beans, healed wounds, and real monsters, so why not the lance?

"Maybe you need to build your strength." I winked.

It was all the time we had to jest. Longinus's roar thundered through the cave. He jabbed a claw through a man's gut and knocked several men against the wall as he had me. When he came toward me, I planted my feet and held the lance in front of me with trembling hands. I waved it back and forth, trying to find an opening to lodge it into his body.

Longinus backed away, cursing, holding his claws in front of his eyes. "It's too bright. Get it away from me."

Longinus stumbled back until he reached the far wall. No light shone from the lance. Then he dropped his arms and snapped his jaw. His expression of rage held me still. Every inch of me quaked and my pulse raced too fast for me to keep up, but I would not show fear.

He snarled. "You dare to threaten me with what was once mine? Where did you get that? Mary took it from me. Did she give it to you?"

The lance was his? Jack and I exchanged glances. I shook my head. Many strange things had happened since the day I first touched the lance, and I had no answers.

"Answer me." Longinus growled and came closer in short time with his long strides, but kept his distance. His breath, smelling of rotting meat, fluttered my hair.

I shuddered and backed away. "I'll answer your question if you tell me where you hid my father."

Longinus glared at me but did not attack. Even as a monster, the need for answers apparently outweighed his thirst for blood. We were born to want questions answered, and curiosity got the best of us all.

"Very well. Back away from the table. If you shine that thing on me, I'll snap your father's neck."

I complied and brought it down. My heart soared.

Father is alive. He's alive. Alive.

Longinus reached with his beastly thick hand behind a curve in the cave wall. Father had been so close and unguarded; why had he not escaped? Happy tears bubbled in my eyes. At last, he would know I kept my promise to come for him.

That feeling burst when Longinus dragged him out, and when I saw him, all of him. Oh, dear God. Oh, God. Oh, God. Oh, God. I nearly fell to my knees.

The loud gasps from the men showed my eyes hadn't played tricks on me. They tried to gather around him, but Longinus stood guard and roared. His paws flung from side to side, and he snapped at us.

"Don't touch him. He's mine." He acted like a child holding

197

on to his favorite toy.

Father's outstretched arm was bound to a thick log, too heavy for his weight, swaying like a drunk as Longinus forced him to walk. His tunic hung in tatters, and fresh claw marks stretched across the front of his chest and back. Dried blood marked his forehead under a wreath of thorns atop his head.

"*Father* did not listen well. He needed some punishment. He would not tell me where you lived. I wanted to reunite your mother and father, but he did not obey," Longinus said casually.

My whole body trembled, as my father's did, but for a different reason. I wanted to kill Longinus. My heart bled with anger, revenge, and hate. No words could describe seeing Father in such horrid condition. It gutted my insides.

Why is this happening? Father is a good kind man. He does not deserve this.

I cursed silently at the world—even God. Then I blamed myself.

Somehow, fate had brought me to this man who had taken me in and loved me as his own daughter. He had taught me how to be strong, and yet I weakened. He had taught me how to love, yet my heart burned with hatred. He had taught me to forgive, yet I wanted to kill Longinus with every essence of my being.

My ugly fate had brought Father there.

Tears streamed down my face, and I had to use every bit of strength I had not to break apart. Father needed me. I must find myself again to save him. Turning away, I wiped the tears so Longinus would not know how badly he hurt me. I did not want to give him the satisfaction.

"I've done as you asked. You pay your end of the bargain, little girl. Where did you get that lance?" Longinus dragged his claws on the ground around my father—a warning.

My fists tightened so hard I felt them go numb, and I let the darkest part of my soul free. "I'm going to kill you," I seethed slowly with venom in my tone. "Then I'm going to kill every member of your crazy family, and not just in this cave. I'm going to make every one of your people burn alive in Hell, the Hell I will create for them."

His half-human, half-lion-like nose twitched as he scraped his claws down the boulder next to him, making long scratch marks. I cringed. It sounded like fingernails on slate. If I didn't know any better I'd thought he was sharpening his claws.

"Isn't that what my people are doing to your people right now?" He moved onto his other claw, doing the same. "Funny how this cycle never ends. Now, speak before I rip your father's heart out."

I circled Longinus, trying to find a way to my father as I spoke, "Oh no. You did not treat my father well. I'm not happy. And when I'm not happy, I tend to change my mind." I rambled on, trying to distract him. When I found an opening, I raised the lance as close to his face as possible. "I will take my father back."

He shrank away and covered his eyes. "Kill them all!"

Strength and speed that were not mine came to me, and the throbbing pain lifted. The lance gave me power.

It had given me visions; why not other abilities? I would question it no more. I accepted the divinity, along with my destiny. My courage rose. The inherited weapon would help me kill

Longinus.

Ten monsters came at us at once, and we scattered. The monsters did not seem to be bothered by the light like Longinus. It did not matter; I fought like a warrior.

I jumped from one small boulder to another and then leapt up two more boulders—each bigger than the last—to give myself height. I stood at the same level as one of the monster's face. Leaping off, I pointed the lance downward and pierced through its heart. It did not drop to the ground in a natural death. Instead, it burst into flames and disappeared as if it had never existed.

It should not have made sense, yet I accepted the lance's power. Nine more to kill to bring my father home.

Out of the corner of my eye, I saw William and his men bring two monsters down to their knees. Then William decapitated them. The dead monsters did not disappear like the one I had killed; they dropped to the ground, and their blood soaked the dirt.

When two monsters came at me at once, I ducked and hid behind a boulder. Their long claws grabbed at me, but the boulder was close to the wall, and their big hands could not reach. Then I stabbed the lance through their palm one after the other. They exploded into fiery dust.

Jack rode one of the monsters like a horse. Leave it to Jack to be crazy, but I loved his craziness. The monster dropped with Jack's dagger sprouting from its head.

Only four monsters left until Father was free. So close. I felt his arms around me.

"Just hold on, Father. I'm coming." My panic and urgency to save father surged me forward.

I jabbed the lance into a monster's foot and then I turned to pierce another. Though I did not injure it gravely, it disappeared in flames. When I spun to find the others, William and his men had taken down two. I readied myself to face the last one, but it slipped away, only to get its belly sliced across by Jack's sword. Blood spilled from the deep slash as it howled in pain and dropped.

Longinus stood not too far, his back to me, swinging his arms at the men, leaving me a clear path to him. With confidence, I threw the lance with every bit of strength I possessed. Watching, I held my breath as the lance soared to stab Longinus in the side just as he turned.

I've got you now. I will be the end of you.

My gloating smile faltered. The lance did not harm him, but instead bounced away. It flew back to me and landed in my hands. I gasped and my blood ran cold. My purpose and certainty deserted me.

Longinus could not be killed.

What was I to do?

Longinus's eyes rounded. Then his malicious amber irises glowed, pulsating. "You cannot kill me. My own lance will not betray me. Even this material thing will not forsake me. How about your God?"

My heart stopped. I had not noticed until that moment Longinus held Father by the arm. For the first time since I had arrived, Father looked at me. His eyes darkened with terror.

Father already looked bad enough, with the dried blood covering him. Having a closer view of his severely battered and bruised face brought me to another level of anger.

Biting my lip and holding my breath, I tried to plot my next move. Not knowing what Longinus had planned, I waited. I would have brandished the lance again, but I worried he would react by hurting Father.

"Throw my lance toward me, carefully, or I'll rip out your father's heart," he said.

Without hesitation, I threw the lance at his feet. He reached down to pick it up, but like Jack, Longinus could not. I was as mystified as he was. Roaring in anger, he stomped back to Father.

Longinus's evil eyes beamed wickedly while his claws drummed on the log tied to Father.

Click. Click. Click.

With every passing moment, my heart pounded faster, awaiting his next move. With a claw, he slit the rope, freeing one of Father's arms. When he cut through the other with another swift slash, Father dropped to his knees, and slumped forward, the log tumbling off to the side.

Father's bloody chest rose and fell rapidly. He might be on his last breath. I closed my eyes, unable to bear what he'd gone through.

I did not realize I was walking toward my father until Jack held me back.

"No. He's trying to lure you in without the lance."

"I need to help Father. He's hurt." Tears formed in my eyes. Reaching out my hand, I murmured, "Father, I am here. I've come back for you just as I promised. You are not alone."

Father slowly tilted up his head. His blackened eyes swelled almost shut, but I knew he could hear me. I needed him to know I had come back for him. When a small smile lifted his lips, which seemed to take much effort, I let out a shuddering cry.

"I'm going to take you out of here," I said. "Mother awaits us at home."

His lips twitched slightly when I mentioned Mother.

"How touching." Longinus gave me mocking grin. "Did you think you could win, little girl?"

"Take me. Let my father go. I'm the one you want. I'm the one who can kill you. I am of Mary's blood. You seek revenge? Take it from my flesh."

He craned his neck sideways. Baffled. Sizing me up. "You would take your father's place? He is not your father. He is not of your blood."

"Yes."

"Why?"

"He *is* my father, whether I am of his blood or not. He is hurting. He needs care. He'll die soon if you don't release him."

I dropped my pride and pleaded. There wasn't anything I wouldn't say or do to help him. I'd thought if Longinus could remember his loved ones, his heart would soften and perhaps he would let Father go.

"Do you remember your family or anyone from your past? Was there anyone you would give your life for?"

"My wife and children."

I was surprised he replied quickly, and even more so when he growled and looked baffled by the fact he had answered me.

His ears, nose, and lips twitched. "They're gone, taken from me. It does not matter."

Every time he spoke, his foul animal breath brushed my face.

"It does matter," I said. "You can't be with them because you're here. Then that's not love. You love yourself more."

"That is not true." He snarled. "I once loved them. I suffered greatly when I turned into this creature and they were taken from me. They were my life." His tone softened, and so did his expression. "It's been a long while since I've thought of them ... my wife and two sons."

"You do not know love." I all but snarled, my temper taking control of my words, my objective forgotten. "If you did, you would not commit this coward's act. How do you think they would feel to see you like this? Would they be proud of you?"

"That's enough! You do not know anything. You think love is the answer? I say hatred is. I will make you feel what I feel. I will do such awful things you will hate me, and your God. You won't believe in anything, and Mary will have failed. You hear me, Mary? You have failed." He tipped his head back and let out a hearty, boisterous laugh. "Just like God abandoned his only son, He will do the same to you. He does not care for you. Let's see if it's true. How fast can you run, little girl?"

No. No. No.

My chest caved in. My plan had backfired.

I shook my head in fear of what Longinus planned to do. Pushing Jack away so he could not stop me, I ran toward my father. Even knowing I was probably going to be too late, I had to do it for the small chance I would reach him in time.

Faster. Run faster. Hurry. Hurry. Hurry. Father, I'm coming for you. Please, God, help me.

Chapter Twenty-Four
Oh, My Heart

"**N**o—" I screamed with every breath in me, hoping to stop him, but instead I watched Longinus drive a claw right through Father's back. He pulled it out just as I reached him.

Oh, my heart, my heart, my heart.

My father arched his back as he let out a sharp gasp and collapsed. Longinus had hurt Father, but he might as well have shredded my soul. I shook with uncontrollable rage.

"How could you?" I shrieked, trying to grasp what had just happened. "You're an evil monster. I hate you!"

His dark lips twitched smugly. "That's it. Hate me, little one. Be angry with me. Say it again."

His smugness intensified my wrath. Longinus lowered his head. He could swallow me whole if he wanted, but he would not. At least not yet.

My jaw clenched, fists hardened like rocks, and I lost control. I fought the throbbing ache that spread through my body, squeezing me tightly. Longinus had trampled my heart and broken my soul.

My breath came short and fast as my chest heaved. "I hate you. I'm going to kill you." A wild growl reverberated from my throat.

"Good. Hate me. Feel that anger. Take it all in. Think about what I did to your father. I stripped him. I beat him until he begged me to stop. I made him suffer. Then I killed him. I enjoyed it. And I would do it again if I could."

I covered my ears. "I hate you. I hate you. I hate you."

I felt hatred to the depth of my marrow and burned through my soul.

"Go ahead and hate me. Hate everyone around you. Hate your God. Hate yourself for not saving your father." He paused for a second, and then with a triumphant, evil grin, said, "I've won."

At his words, I dropped to my father and sobbed. I had let darkness take me over completely, empty me out, and swallow me whole. And seeing Father on the ground, soaked in blood, I knew Longinus was right.

I had no fight left in me. He might as well kill me. I would let him. But thoughts of Mother carried me on. I had to fight for her.

My moan echoed through the cave.

Longinus was right. I knew agony. I knew pain. My lungs could not handle the gasps as I panted and wailed. Tears poured as I scooped Father's head in my arms and briefly studied his battered face.

I searched for hints of the way he was before. When I could not find him, I got angrier. My eyes shifted to his punctured stomach, blood pooling around him and streaming down from the corner of his mouth. So much blood.

I had failed him.

"Father, I am here. You're not alone." I brought his bloody hand to my cheek and wept harder. "I'm going to kill him. I'm going to avenge your death. I swear on my life I will."

Longinus growled, but he didn't carry out his threat.

Warm hands rested on my shoulders. I knew them to be Jack. When Father coughed up blood, I was shocked to know he was alive. I leaned lower when he parted his lips.

"No, Jaclyn," Father said weakly. "You have a destiny to fulfill, as I have just fulfilled mine. Hatred does not win over evil. Only love and forgiveness can." He paused. Every word he spoke dragged out slowly and took great effort. "Promise me you'll forgive Longinus. It's the only way."

"No, Father." I shook my head vigorously.

How could he ask me such a thing? Every breath became a battle. My soul and will had been drowned in hatred. Only the will to fight fired in me, and I had no love to give to the evil monster who deserved to burn in Hell.

"Yes, Jaclyn. He needs to know love, and that there's hope again. He must know he can be forgiven."

"I will not, Father." I sobbed harder.

Tears blinded me. My head throbbed, and my body trembled under the weight of the ache eating me alive. I had never known such pain, or such hatred.

When the one you love is leaving you, all the times you spent together, good and bad, run through your mind. The first time Father had lifted me and placed me on his shoulder to pick an apple from the apple tree. How he had taught me to use a weapon. The first time he had put me on a horse. All the wisdom he had preached I would cherish, all the tears he had to wipe, and even when he had scolded me—he showed me love.

"Father, Father. Please don't leave me," I whimpered.

"Even in death, I'll never leave you. Find me in your heart. Promise me you'll forgive him for he knows not what he does. It's my last request."

"I will. I promise."

"Harden not your heart, Jaclyn. Love is the only way. Remember my words, Jaclyn."

I did recall clearly. *If you can forgive the flaws and see the beauty, then it is saved. Forgive and show love. It is the only way to save and to be saved. Lead with love in your heart. Then you shall shine through the deepest darkness.*

"Tell your mother I love her very much, that I tried to come home." Tears trickled down the side of his face. He coughed again, his body trembling and his hand so cold. "I'll carry you in my heart always." Father inhaled a sharp, deep breath. "She's beautiful. She's..." Then ... he took his last breath.

I'd heard when a righteous person dies, someone from their past leads them to the light of Heaven. My father had just seen his angel. He was going home.

"Father." Tears streamed like a waterfall. "Father ... Father!" My cry poured through my heart and soul as I wrapped my arms around him. "Why?" I howled out again. "I was supposed to bring you home. How am I going to face Mother? How are we going to live without you?"

All this time, Longinus held a victorious grin as he watched me suffer. I wondered when he would strike me down.

I wanted to hate Longinus. I wanted to drive the lance through his heart. But I had promised Father, and I would break myself to fulfill his last request.

I had no idea what to do next. My will had been spent, and it took everything in me not to lose faith, but I had to do it, for Father. I did not want his death to have been in vain.

Letting go of Father, I closed his eyes. "May you find peace. I will see you one day."

Without any reason or thought, I dug my nails into the dirt so hard my knuckles turned white. I wanted so badly to kill Longinus and give him as much pain as he had given me. But instead I crawled to face him with my head down, as if bowing before a king.

He had sent his monsters to butcher our innocent people. He didn't deserve forgiveness, or salvation. But perhaps he couldn't see beyond revenge because he had been so heartless, soulless, and close-minded for so long, and there was no one to help him see the light.

Was I to be the one?

I desperately fought against the violent demon inside me, wanting to burst. But what about Longinus? What was he thinking? Perhaps scheming some form of torture for me, since he had not killed me yet.

"What are you doing?" Jack tried to pick me up. "We need to get out of here while we have the chance."

I looked Jack squarely in the eyes. "I need to do this, please."

I had hardly any strength left. Exhausted, watching Father's life slip away before me, my body had shut down, but a new clarity blossomed inside me, and I knew what I had to say.

Mother's words sang in my head. *Everyone has a story to tell. We'll see what lies ahead for you. Fate will lead you to a path you are meant to take.*

I knew what I had to do, magic or no magic. I must live my own story.

Jack backed away, directing his father and the men to leave. I wanted Jack to leave, too, but I had no voice left to tell him, and I knew no matter what I'd said, he would not abandon me.

My voice did not sound like my own in my dry, hoarse throat as I sobbed. "I forgive you, Longinus." Those three words broke whatever amount of tiny spirit I had left. They were the hardest words I'd ever spoken. But I carried on for Father, because it was his last request. "You do not know what you do. You're bleeding in anger, vengeance, and hate. Let your heart be free so you can be free. I forgive you."

When he did not speak, I peered up at him. His eyes widened and went wild in confusion.

"No." He shook his head. "What do you mean? You mustn't forgive me." Cold anger filled his eyes. "How could you? I killed your father. You should hate me. You should want revenge. Your heart should be as cold as mine." Still in disbelief, he continued to gape at me.

I rose and took a step toward him. "My heart is not yours. I don't hate you. I feel sorry for you."

"No. Stay away from me." Longinus placed out his hand as if that could stop me.

"I forgive you, Longinus."

He stumbled back farther. "No, you don't. You hate me. You can't forgive me. I don't want it. I murdered your father before you."

Picking up the lance, I readied it with the tip toward him. With every word spoken, I took a step as he backed away and covered his eyes.

"Free yourself, Longinus. It's time. You and your people have suffered enough. I know you have love and good in your heart because you care for your people. Let them free for eternity; if not for yourself, then for them. Look at what you've done. You sent your people out to kill those who have nothing to do with your revenge. They don't know you. They don't understand you, but I do. Let it go."

"I won't."

"Release your hatred."

"No." He growled.

"Release your anger."

"Stop!"

"Release your sadness."

"Never!"

"Release your thirst for revenge. Think about your wife and children. They miss you. They love you. They need you. They want to see you."

He paused, looking tormented. "Jane, Matthew, Mark?" he murmured under his breath, reaching toward the lance I held in front of him.

Through the magic of the lance, he too saw his family, as I had. His irises flickered between amber and blue, then blue to amber, wavering as if they could not make up their mind.

"Jane, Matthew, and Mark are waiting for you. Ask for forgiveness. It's the only way to set yourself free so you can go

211

home. Find love in your heart again. Go home to your wife and children. What are you doing here, suffering for all these years?"

"Home?" His tone softened for the first time and he said the word as if it was foreign.

"Open up your heart and let me in. That is all I ask."

Longinus dropped to his knees and covered his ears. "Forgive. It hurts. Forgive. My head hurts. My heart hurts. Forgive. Stop it. Forgive me. No—"

"You're feeling what was once good in your soul. Find it again. Ask for forgiveness from your heart." I brought the spear in front of his face.

"Stop. I … I…" He curled his body into a ball, tucking his knees to his chest.

In his monster form, he still looked bigger than life. Rocking back and forth, he shouted out names and the word, "Forgive." He babbled senseless things like the devil had taken over his mind.

I put distance between us, afraid of the unknown and what would become of Longinus. Would he burst into flames? Would he grab for me? The lance couldn't kill him as I'd thought, making the light emitting from the lance my weapon.

Longinus was still in his beast form and had not changed. I had to continue, do something. He had to know God still cared. Though my heart was troubled for different reasons than his, we both had to let go of this deep binding hatred and revenge.

Reaching deep into my faith, I said the words we both needed to hear. "When you feel completely hopeless, let me be your light."

"No, you cannot. I don't want this." He groaned as though he was in pain, twisting from side to side.

212

"When you are too blinded to see, I will be your eyes."

His body thrashed, and he slammed his head on the boulder beside him over and over, as if that would prevent him from hearing my voice. As blood trickled down his forehead, he punched the boulder, one blow after another. Crimson liquid seeped through the open cuts.

"When your will has been broken, I will be your strength. And when you've been swallowed up by darkness, I will be your light and hold you tight and never let go."

Longinus released a guttural, animal cry and began to claw at the wall as if to climb it. Fragments of rock showered down as he dug. Then his dagger-sharp talons began to rake his chest and face, tearing through his hair and flesh. Crimson liquid seeped through the gashes and painted the dirt.

I didn't know if my sermon got through to him in a way I'd hoped. It certainly drove him frantic, so I preached on. "As Jesus sacrificed himself for his people, so must you do the same for yours." I squared my shoulders and held my chin high. "I am Jaclyn, Richard's daughter, descendant of Mary, and a child of God. I will be the salvation you seek. Be at peace and repent of your evil ways."

With every word, I took a step closer to Longinus. With every word, my father's love and peace overfilled me. With every word, tears streamed down my face. And with every word I felt my own words mending my heart, freeing me from my own hatred and grief.

Warmth I'd never felt before wrapped around my soul, as if love was a physical presence, and I didn't feel so alone. And I wondered if Longinus felt the same.

Something was happening to Longinus. The only way he could change into human form was to sacrifice a sheep and drink a cup of its blood, but he hadn't. As he shrank smaller, his claws recoiled into his paws, and his paws became his own hands and feet.

The black and brown animal hair began to shed at the same time, his face twisted and contorted. When the transformation finally ended, Longinus had turned fully human.

Longinus extended his arms with his head thrown back. "Forgive me. My life is Yours. Do as You will. Deliver me from evil."

As soon as he spoke, the scar on his face and birthmarks on my wrists became as bright as the rising sun. Light penetrated my boots from the birthmarks on my feet. The lance vibrated in my hands— a forewarning.

Holding my breath, I awaited the unknown. Then the lance shot out from my hands and drove itself into Longinus's left side.

At the impact, the illuminating beams from my birthmarks faded and molten-gold light glowed around Longinus, blinding me. The light flickered in colors of orange and yellow like a living flame. It did not seem possible, but his body, with the lance still lodged in his ribs, burst into fire from the inside.

After a few seconds, flames engulfed him as he smiled at me. A soft, happy, thankful smile. Then Longinus disappeared amid a flurry of ash and embers. The monsters lying dead on the ground also burst into flames.

I hoped the same happened to those still ravaging the towns.

"Thank you." His voice, human and softened with humility,

floated on the air.

I wondered if the others had heard it, too.

"May God have mercy on your soul," I breathed.

Finally, it ended.

With Longinus's salvation, I knew our people were safe too.

I dropped to the floor. Great shudders of relief racked me, and I held my arms to my chest. Then I realized the ground shook, not I. The cave quaked harder by the second.

Small boulders the size of melons fell from above and crashed near me. As I threw my arms over my head, the ground started caving beneath me.

"It's time to go," Jack said urgently.

Snapping out of my daze, I stood, and ran with him as he held my hand. My cloudy mind slowed my movements and made me clumsy. I was thankful Jack looked after me. William's men were gone and so were the sheep, but William stood in the distance, beckoning us with a wave of his hand.

"My father. I need to get his body." I yanked my hand from Jack and ran the other way.

"It's too late." He ran after me.

I gasped as I stopped. The whole chunk of ground where Father lay had vanished. Oh, my heart. I did not think anyone could take so much pain in one day.

"I needed to say goodbye one last time. I wanted to bury him at our home, where he belonged. I wanted to bring him home. You could have at least given me that," I cried, as if God could hear me.

God had taken my father's life and his body, leaving me nothing of him. I wanted to curse at Him, but it was not my place, for the Bible said we do not belong to ourselves but to God alone. He gives us life, and He can take it as well.

I'd learned that though we can love our family and friends, they do not truly belong to us. We fulfill our predestined fates, and then it is our time to go.

"I'm sorry, Jaclyn. We'll give him a burial, I promise." Jack took my hand again.

I ran faster, jumping over the breaking ground and dodging the falling rocks.

Fear drove me to madness as the walls began to collapse. My legs buckled as I ran over the shaking ground.

Mother needed me. She could not lose both of us. Thoughts of her drove me on.

I crossed the wooden bridge just as flames began licking the other side, and I ran toward the bit of blue sky visible at the end of the cave. Finally, I inhaled fresh air.

The sun peeked through the clouds and warmth bathed me. I had no time to waste. I jumped, wrapped my arms and legs around the beanstalk and plummeted with Jack behind me.

Once again, the beanstalk caught fire just as I was halfway down. William's men had already chopped down most of the leaves on their way down, giving us a clear path to drop at great speed.

William's men mounted their horses and had ours ready. Twenty people had come to Black Mountain, not counting William, Jack, and myself, but only seven of us were leaving. I silently thanked the men who had given their lives to save so many others, and hoped they would see my father in Heaven so he could thank them, too.

I jumped on Angel and took off. The collapsed cave created a cloud of massive dust, and the mountain itself started to crumble and sink into the earth. No evidence of the Black Mountain would remain.

My heart hurt, and perhaps always would, knowing Father's body had been buried inside the mountain, but it was out of my control. Following an impulse, I reached inside my boot, took out the last bean, and threw it far toward the mountain.

I never wanted to need or see the bean again.

The earth continued to rumble beneath me as I rode off as fast as Angel could carry me. Thunderous, roaring sounds of rocks crashing echoed after me as I burst out of the forest. I passed through the town where Jack and I had saved the family with twins. I hoped they were alive and well.

I saw no more monsters—only people working together to clean up. They would eventually rebuild, because that is what people do. Some fires still smoldered, but most of the flames had died.

I traveled all day and late into the night. The stars were out, illuminating the night like white fire, the brightest I'd ever seen. Father used to say the stars were angels' eyes watching over us. Surely, he was right. God showed He was happy by gracing us with holy lights.

The six lanterns hanging from the horses ahead of me stood out in the darkness as we made the last turn for home. I smelled Mother's vegetable soup and freshly baked bread, and felt her love wrap around me.

How do I tell her about Father?

217

Jack and I rode side by side together, silently. Occasionally, he glanced my way but did not speak. I twitched, startled to see William pull his horse up next to mine.

"I'm sorry about your father," he said somberly. "He was a great man and a wonderful friend."

I bit my lip to stop the tears. "Thank you. And thank you for risking your life to help him."

"You were raised by a brave man so you could become who you are today. He has fulfilled his destiny, so do not mourn him. Instead, rejoice, for he is home. This is not goodbye."

I nodded with a smile.

William pulled out something from the side pocket of his saddle. "I found this when I went back to the prison to look for him. I knew you would want to have it."

"Thank you." I held out a hand and took the hat.

William nudged his horse forward to ride with his men.

I hugged Father's hat tightly to my chest as if I were holding him. I inhaled the sweat from his hard labor; it also smelled like home and love. To William, it was just Father's hat, but to me, it was everything.

Unable to stop myself any longer, I sobbed into the hat, pouring out my grief.

This hat holds a special place in my heart. I've had this hat since the day you blessed my life. It holds a wonderful memory of you. I shall hold it forever and carry it with me wherever I go, as I carry you in my heart always.

And I will always carry you in my heart, Father.

Chapter Twenty-Five
Home At Last.

other ran out the door, along with Jonathas and four other men. They must have heard the horses. The house and barn showed no sign of monsters. Another blessing. The men greeted each other and chatted among themselves.

"Jaclyn." Mother embraced me and pulled back to stroke my hair, my face, and kiss my cheek. "Are you well? Are you hurt? You look so filthy. Is that blood?" She laughed and happy tears pooled in her eyes. She gazed past me, looking for Father with eager eyes, I assumed.

"William, Jack, and gentlemen." She nodded to greet them and received nods in return. "It's good to see you well. There are so few of you." Mother turned to me with lips trembling. "Where's Richard?" Her forehead creased, tiny wrinkles I had never seen before forming by her eyes.

I needed no words. I showed her Father's hat, and the tears streaming down my face told the rest of the story.

"I'm so sorry," I whispered, unable to meet her gaze.

I sobbed harder.

Coming home alone without Father, guilt ate through my soul. There were no words of comfort to lessen the pain. I had shattered her world.

"No." She whimpered softly, folding her arms. "It can't be true." Mother grabbed my arms and shook me. "Jaclyn, tell me it is not true. Where's your father?" When I didn't answer, she turned to William. "Where's my Richard? Where's my Richard? You told me you would bring him home. You promised."

William dropped his head and held his hat to his heart.

"Mother." I touched her lightly on the shoulder. "Father is in Heaven."

"No." Mother dropped to the ground, gasping for air. "No, no, no. Why did God take him from me? He's a good man."

I wrapped my arms around her and held her tightly.

I'm so sorry, Mother. I'm so sorry I failed to bring Father home, your husband you love so dearly.

Guilt clawed through my soul and nothing I said or did would ever fix this.

I'd cried so much I had no tears left to shed, but Mother's tears were fresh. She mourned loud enough for the both of us, her body shuddering. She yelled out and wept until she had nothing left in her, while the men grieved silently, standing around us with their heads bowed. Then, after some time, Mother stood up and wiped her tears.

"Where are my manners?" Mother held open the door as if nothing had happened, but her lips quivered, and her puffy eyes glistened in tears. "Gentlemen, please come in. I've made soup and fresh bread. You must be starving." She opened the door and waited until everyone entered.

The smell of Mother's cooking drove my stomach to fold on

itself, but food was the last thing on my mind. While everyone sat around to eat, I went to my chamber, placed Father's hat on my bed, and changed into clean clothes.

The smell of sweat, burnt beans, and old, dried blood on my clothes made me want to vomit. Just as I finished, Mother entered my room. I caught Mother's teary eyes and then her smile. She sat on the bed, embraced me, and rubbed a small idle circle on my back. When she pulled away, she held my hands.

"I'm so proud of you. I tease you for wearing boy clothes and for not acting like a lady, but I'm your mother and I must help you find the right husband who will love you and take care of you, just like your father did for me." She whimpered softly and looked down when she mentioned Father.

Her tears dropped between our clasped hands, and I held my breath and bit my lip.

You needn't be strong with me, Mother. Let me be your shoulder to cry on. Share your grief and suffering with me. Let me carry your burden for once.

After a few long seconds, she looked back at me. "Your father loved you very much. I know you know this, but I have to say it. He's very proud of you for being so brave. I don't think any other girl would have chased danger like you did. I don't know what happened on the mountain today, and I hope you'll tell me when we are alone. I want to know everything, even the details of your father's death. I need to know." Her hands tightened around mine.

"Of course," I said, my throat aching.

My mother, who just learned her husband passed, held strong. *Women have their own bravery,* Mother had said before. She'd proved it many times and I knew Father was proud of her too.

"Please come out and eat." Mother smiled. She caressed my face and went back out to be the good hostess.

A soft knock on the door roused me from thoughts of Father, and I brushed the tears lingering from my eyes before they could fall.

"Come in." My dry, cracking voice did not sound like my own.

The door opened.

Jack walked in with a bowl of soup and a cup of water, and then closed the door behind him. He gazed up and down my body with his eyebrows arched and his lips pursed. "You're wearing a dress?"

"It was the only thing clean to wear." I shrugged. It was a simple blue dress, but the expression on Jack's face made me feel naked.

"You look ... lovely." His face beamed under the lantern light.

Our eyes locked for some time until he cleared his throat.

"I thought you would rather eat in your chamber." He looked at the items he held.

"Thank you, but I have no desire to eat, but I'll drink." I took the cup from his hand and took a sip, and then reached over to place it on the table next to my bed.

"You may not be, but your stomach is troubled. I hear it calling, 'feed me, feed me.'" He brought the bowl closer. "Open up."

"Jack." I laughed softly. Pressing my lips together, I leaned back, and then sat straight when he moved the bowl away. "I can feed myself, and my stomach said no such words."

"True, but you must eat. What you did back at the mountain, I cannot begin to understand it. You were so brave and strong. I know you don't want to hear it, but I am truly sorry for your loss. Your heart is sad, and your soul worn, but comfort will come. This storm will pass and the sun will shine again, for I will make it so. I shall keep my word until my last breath. You are my hero, Jaclyn."

"Thank you, but I am no hero. And I have no words to praise myself. God has not forsaken us as Longinus once thought. In the end, He showed his love and grace by saving us all through you and everyone who went to Black Mountain. God doesn't show himself but rather works through people. I was his vessel, his weapon. I was the nail to Longinus's cross. It was my fate, my father's, yours, and everyone that went to Black Mountain. I am saddened so many had to perish. Their loss fills me with grief."

Jack placed the bowl down and sat next to me. "I feel the same, Jacky. I'm glad 'tis over."

"Aye," I muttered softly, looking at my grimy fingers.

Dried blood caked my hand, my father's blood, and dirt rimmed my fingernails, so I curled my fingers to hide them.

Jack rested his hand on mine. "Don't be ashamed of honest dirt. Ladies are to be proper and clean, but you are more than that. You're stubborn like your horse. And you have a temper."

I raised my eyebrows.

He continued. "You do as you will. You say unladylike words. And you fight like a man. But I like you just as you are. You're beautiful, Jaclyn, body and soul. Why do you think you were the one who saved our people? No one who didn't see it will believe a girl saved us, but the men out there know. You're special, a rare jewel, one of a kind, don't you ever forget that."

I blinked in shock. Jack's words touched the depths of my soul. Smiling, I shyly dipped my chin.

"Thank you." The words escaped softly, timidly.

He passed me the bowl. "Please eat. I must go, but I aim to be back in three days to help with the funeral. I know there's no body, but we can say words. I'll get Father Michael from the other town to say a mass. I'm not too fond of Father Henry."

"Thank you." I smiled again, his kind words filling me.

Jack got up and opened the door.

"Jack?"

He spun. "Yes?"

"You can call me Jacky."

His face lit up like the moon. "Are you sure?"

"Yes. And … and—"

"Yes."

I held up his mother's cloak. "I should give this back to you. I'll wash it first. There's some blood stain on it."

He regarded the cloak for a moment and gave a faint, honest grin. "It would be my honor if you kept it."

"But your father might—"

"He would be honored too. He knew you wore Mother's cloak. He would have said something to me if he had disapproved. Besides, my mother loved cloaks. She had bundles."

I didn't know what to say. A part of me felt honored he would give me something that belonged to his beloved mother, but a part of me felt I didn't deserve it.

"Are you sure?"

224

"More than you know."

"Then I'll take good care of it and wear it with pride."

He placed a hand to his chest and bowed, and that was his answer.

I called his name when he turned to leave.

"Yes," he chortled.

I shrugged sheepishly. "Bless you. Thank you for your kindness and friendship." My eyes pooled with tears. "I do not know how I would have made it without you."

I'd pretended I didn't need him in the cave, and perhaps I had been harsh with him, but I was afraid he thought I couldn't hold my own. I didn't want to come across as someone weak and fragile.

His chest rose and fell with a sigh. "It was my pleasure. But Jaclyn …" He cleared his throat. "I mean Jacky, I am not your friend."

My mouth fell open. After all we'd been through together, and after all those words that had poured lovingly from the very lips I wanted to kiss … How could I have been so wrong about him?

Before I recovered enough to give him a piece of my mind, and maybe even a punch in the face, he said, "I am not just your friend because I want to be your life-long and best friend." With a wink, he closed the door behind him.

My heart leapt and my smile spread. I'd fallen a little bit in love with him right at that moment. After gulping down the rest of the water I desperately needed, I finished the soup as my mind drifted to memories of Father.

Chapter Twenty-Six
Three Days Later

ack kept his promise. He dug a small hole at the back of the house to bury the hat I had bought at the market. With no body to bury, I thought the hat represented Father well. I'd contemplated burying his old hat, but I decided to keep it and placed it on top of my chest.

We placed a large wooden cross over the disturbed earth. Father would have been pleased, but to me, it seemed too little.

I gave Mother the brush and the handheld mirror I'd traded for a silver piece at the market. After I explained the reason, she hugged me and cried.

I did not expect the crowd of people from all over town. And to see them dressed in black—men, women, and even children— humbled me. Many who had known my father came to pay their last respects. Their generous gifts surprised me the most. Some gave us coins, meals, fabrics, cattle, sheep, chickens, and much more.

My heart overflowed with gratefulness for their love and support. Quite a few men offered to help around the farm, and Mother and I accepted. We were strong women, but we needed help.

After Father Michael finished the ceremony, everyone left except for Jack's family. I went to my room to change and take a moment to myself. All the condolences and tear-shedding had exhausted me. Some had even thanked me and kissed my cheek; I assumed they knew what happened at the Black Mountain.

Jack's family stayed for dinner, helped us clean up, and then departed. Mother and I were grateful.

***

One Month Later

Jack's family came to visit us in the afternoon. His father and his brothers had momentarily stepped out with my mother to the barn. The barn door had slightly unhinged and needed fixing. I sat at the dining table for a moment, a brief respite between chores.

Jack strode in and gave me a crooked smile.

I flattened my lips to keep from smiling.

"How are you?"

I smoothed out my dress and met his gaze. "I'm fine. Thank you for asking."

"I know it's a bit soon, but when you are ready, I would like to ask for your hand in marriage."

My cheeks flushed and I swallowed too fast. "You … you want to marry me?"

Jack came around to my side of the table and sat beside me. "Yes." He placed a gently hand on my hand.

Like lightning, tingles shot though every inch of me. How could he make me feel like that with a touch? A shiver ran through me when he caressed my thumb with his, as faint as a ghost touch.

I wasn't sure whether it was all in my head.

"When you're ready and if you're willing, I shall claim you as my bride."

Jack was a good man, and my heart swelled when I thought of him. Slowly, I drew my hand back but returned his steady gaze. I did not know what would happen if he continued to hold my hand.

"And if I will not go with you? What if I say no?" I bit the inside of my cheek when he leaned closer. Having him so close made me dizzy, but it got worse when he dipped his head. *Oh heavens.*

"Then I guess I'd have to convince you." Jack's warm breath brushed against my neck.

"How?" I breathed. Anticipation traced through my limbs as fast as Angel's stride.

"Like this." He lips met mine, so soft and gentle.

Trembling, I blinked and held myself immobile. I barely drew breath or moved to protest. I'd never kissed a man before.

But then, something burst inside of me. I no longer denied the attraction between us. Stars shone upon me and Heaven opened to angels singing. Twisting my lips from his, I drew in a ragged breath.

Jack pulled back, raking his fingers through his hair. His eyes twinkled. "Convinced?" He sighed. "I should go help my fathers. I mean my brothers. My father and brother ... brothers."

I giggled at his rambling.

Then he stumbled out the door, leaving me breathless.

I placed my fingertip to my mouth, feeling the ghost of Jack's lips upon mine again. My heart hammered as I released a quivering breath. It had been my first kiss, and Jack was the only man I ever wanted to kiss me again. I was sure of it. After what we'd been through, I knew he was the one.

Funny how I never thought I would find a mate, and he had been there all along.

Chapter Twenty-Seven
The Proposal

A year had passed since we'd laid Father to rest. My heart was still broken and my soul crushed. Every day I prayed Father rested in Heaven, and every day I thought about our precious time together, those years I'd thought would last much longer.

I also wondered about Longinus. I wished him well as I could, but sometimes I wished he burned in Hell. I spent more time in prayer for those thoughts, but I would never forget he killed my father.

The tortured cries no longer haunted me at nights. I had been freed. Born from Mary Magdalene's line, my destiny had been fulfilled. Despite Father's death, I felt thankful for all the goodness in my life.

Mother and I tended the animals and the farm together. It was a lot of hard work, but it kept us busy, kept us moving forward without Father. At busy times, friends would stop by to help. In turn, Mother would cook them delicious meals.

Sometimes it felt like Father died yesterday, and other times it felt like it happened an eternity before. Some days it hurt so much, it ached to breathe.

On good days, Mother and I would talk about Father, the silly and funny things he'd done, and on bad days we held each other and wept. But the nights when Mother whimpered alone in the dark, behind closed doors, pierced my heart.

I buried my grief, loud and fierce as hers, under the covers. Shivering, I would cry until I shed my last tear, so weakened from a broken heart, I would fall asleep. People said I would forget the pain, but I think I just learned to bear it. Mother and I moved on the best we could.

I had told Mother everything that had happened on Black Mountain. She gasped and cried as I told her the truth, and I left out no detail. I even told her the secret Father had shared—how they had become my parents.

She apologized many times, like Father had, and I told her the same thing I had told him: it did not matter. They had raised me as their own.

I was most surprised when Mother told me something new about my past. A piece of paper with my name scribbled on it and the small brush with vines had been inside the basket with me. Then I thought about the witch and what she had said to me.

You look like your mother.

Had she known my mother? Had I known then what I had since learned, I would have asked her more questions, but I supposed some things were better left unknown.

I wondered who my real parents were and why they had to give me up. Mother and I concluded my birth mother must not have been wed when she was pregnant with me. I would have been born out of wedlock and maybe she hadn't wanted that for me, or for herself.

231

I also wondered which of my birth parents were of Mary Magdalene's bloodline and whether they healed like me. That mystery would never be solved unless we found each other someday. I'd not hold my breath for answers.

Some nights I told Mother stories to entertain her, like when Father still lived. And when I thought my heart mended, tears would begin to fall, and it would hurt, like Father had just died. At those times I had to crawl into bed and try to think of something happy, like Jack.

Jack had told me he would come for me when I was ready for him, but he showed up often to help around the farm. He was polite and a perfect gentleman. He stayed for dinner and left. But, of course he stole a kiss or two, here and there.

When I'd finally told Mother about Jack, she said she already knew from the way he looked at me and from the way we could not stop staring at each other when he came around to help. She'd had an intuition we would be together, because he'd always been fond of me.

"Do you think I'm wearing the right dress?" I yawned as Mother braided my hair.

Wanting to have plenty of time to get ready, I'd woken up earlier to do my chores. Jack had said he would arrive in the morning. I just did not know the time.

"It's beautiful on you. Pink goes well with your skin." Mother handed me a mirror.

I returned it to her after I took a look and blew out a breath. "I cannot believe I'm wearing a dress for a man."

"I knew you would when the right man came along." Mother

giggled, placing my dove gray cape around me. "There. You're ready to go. Let me look at you."

I spun around, feeling like a princess. I almost gagged at such a thought. Jack's eyes would flame, and his lips would curl wickedly when he saw me. Maybe he would kiss me more than he should. And ... I stopped such thoughts dwelling in my mind.

"Oh, Jaclyn. I wish your father could see you." Mother's eyes gleamed and she clasped her hands together.

My heart stung at the thought. "I'm sure Father is not smiling right now, Mother. He's telling me to take it off. He's scolding Jack for—" I stopped. I did not want to confess that Jack's and my lips had touched. And oh, how my mind wandered to those moments. "I mean, well, because Father was very protective of me."

Mother smoothed the crinkles on my dress. "That he was."

A knock at the door startled me.

"I'll get it." Mother left my bedroom door slightly ajar, giving me just enough space to peek. "Jack. You look so handsome. Come in." She opened the door wider. "Jaclyn will be out soon. Seat yourself." When she closed the door, she saw me looking. Smiling, she waved for me to come.

I watched Jack in silence, observing him from head to toe. This was Jack—the Jack I'd known since childhood, the Jack who had seen me smeared with dirt and blood, who'd comforted me, stood by me through hard times, and who would have traded his life to save mine.

My heart pattered like heavy raindrops. Mother was right—I would wear a dress for the right man.

Jack's hair was tied back, showing off his fine features and clean-shaven face. His blue hat and tunic and dark pants shone with the finest quality and brought out his green eyes. With the black cloak around him to finish his outfit, he looked fine, polished, and quite the catch.

Taking in a deep breath, I walked out. "Good day, Jack."

Jack jumped up and caught my eyes. His smile stretched to the ceiling as he gazed over the length of me, making my cheeks warm.

"Jacky—pardon me, Jaclyn. You look—" He looked at Mother and cleared his throat. "You look very lovely."

"Thank you," I said. "Shall we go?"

While Mother got up to open the door for us, Jack whispered, "You look beautiful and so delicious."

I giggled just as Mother walked out and turned to us.

"Jack. You know what I wish. One night and that is all." Mother held out her index finger for emphasis.

Jack tipped his hat.

Mother made him do the sign of the cross and promise God. I laughed softly behind Jack. But what was Mother's intention?

"Be safe. Godspeed." Mother caressed my hair, her loving eyes on mine.

I kissed her cheek and smiled. "I shall be back soon."

I worried about Mother being alone.

As if Jack could hear my thoughts, he said to Mother, "My father and brothers will come for a visit."

"I'll look forward to it." She curtsied.

My worries disappeared.

Jack wrapped his arms around my waist, helped me up onto my seat, and whistled for the horses to get moving. I waved at

Mother and looked over my shoulder to see a large, brown blanket covering the wagon.

"What do you have in the wagon?"

"A dead body."

I slapped his arm.

He curled his body like an injured man. "Don't hurt the hand that will feed you and provide for you."

"I can feed and provide for myself." I scoffed.

Jack chuckled. "Then do not hurt the hand that will give you pleasure."

My face flushed. That shut me up for a moment. "Where are we going?"

He gave me a sideways glance with a mischievous grin. "You'll see."

After we rode a long while, Jack stopped and reached under the blanket to bring out a basket full of food. We continued on our path as we ate. He'd packed bread, cheese, cooked chicken, fresh carrots, and apricots.

Apricots were expensive, and I hadn't had them in a while, so I ate them eagerly and gave Jack a kiss for his trouble. He still refused to let me see what other things lurked under the blanket, no matter how much I begged.

"How many children?" Jack asked.

"What?" I almost choked on the apricot. "Who says I'd bear your child?" I giggled. "And why would I?"

"Because we'll have fun making them?"

Oh, heavens.

Why did he have to make me blush all the time? I drank from

235

the jug, hoping it would cool me off, and then offered him some. After he took a gulp, he set the jug between us.

"How many would you like?" I asked.

"We're having two boys and two girls." He chewed on dried meat.

"Really? And I suppose you've already named them."

"I have." He nodded with a grin. "Our firstborn son shall be named after your father, Richard."

My eyes pooled with tears, and I placed my hand over Jack's arm, letting him know how much that meant to me. "'Tis perfect."

He rewarded me with a smile. "Our second son shall be named after my brother, Jeremiah, who passed away."

My mouth parted. "You had a brother who died?"

"It happened when my mother gave birth to him, but that was many years ago."

"Oh, I'm so sorry. I did not know."

It did not matter how many years passed, the pain of loss remained. Ten years hence, I would still remember Father and the agony of losing him.

He dipped his head once in understanding. "Our first daughter shall be named after my mother, Elizabeth. And our second daughter shall be named after the most beautiful woman in the whole world, whom I absolutely adore."

I cocked an eyebrow. "Who?" I hadn't meant to raise my voice at him, so I shoved some cheese into my mouth.

"Why, Jacky, do I detect a tone of jealousy? I think I like it." He smirked.

"Nay, you did not." I gazed at the trees, chewing faster.

"We will name her Jaclyn."

I swallowed and slowly turned to him with a huge smile. "I think you have chosen wisely with all of their names, especially the last one."

I enjoyed the humor between us, but I knew he meant what he had said. I fell in love with him even more. He said and acted proper like a gentleman. He had proved over and over he was genuine.

On our way, we passed through the market town. One year had made quite a difference. Some shops were restored and open for business, while others had some work to be done, wood frames of the unfinished structures scattered through the town. The stores appeared bigger and better.

It was good to see people walking along the road with their families, smiling as if monsters had never come. Peace and harmony filled the town, filling my heart with joy. I gazed at the spot where I'd seen the old woman with beans. She wasn't there, of course, but there was a bean vendor there, by an odd twist of fate.

I'd told Jack about the old woman, but we could not figure out who she was, only that she was a miracle. Jack declared some miracles were unexplainable, like me.

"Mother, look. It's that man and woman who saved us."

I recognized the girl twin from that night. She wore a blue dress and two long braids rested down her front.

"He's the one that gave us money." She pointed at Jack.

The father was bargaining over chickens when the little girl noticed us. My heart leaped with joy to see them alive and well. I thought Jack would stop, but he kept moving. He waved, and I got a chance to see them, but I wondered why he was in such a hurry. And why had the little girl said he'd given them money?

Curiosity burned in my mind, but I decided not to ask. He would tell me when he was ready.

After we passed the town, I'd thought we'd stop soon, but we did not. I trusted Jack, so I did not question him until the road split and he pointed the wagon toward Black Mountain. I waited for him to rest, but as we neared the forest with no sign of returning, anxiety wavered through me and I had to know.

"Where are we going? Why are we going this way? You know it's toward Black Mountain. I don't want to go that way." The panic in my voice grew with each question.

"Jacky." He reached for my hand. "I want to show you something, and I promise it won't be scary. There are no monsters. It's different. I've been wanting to show you, but I wanted to wait until I thought you might be ready."

"Show me what? Please, I need to know before you take me there."

"I don't need to tell you anymore. Look." He tilted his head.

What materialized was impossible, spellbinding me to the heart and soul of the forest. Vast, rolling hills and lush green pastures painted the land. Almond-brown trees reached to the sky, and their roots twisted in knots spurting out from the dirt from their massive size.

Lavender weeping willows swayed to the soft warm breeze like a dance of glory. Birds sang a symphony of love songs, beckoning me farther in as they fluttered from branch to branch, while squirrels scuttled along the trunks.

Patches of flowers I'd never seen before, no doubt magical, spread a yellow, red, blue, and purple carpet beneath me, and soft moss cushioned the wheels of the wagon. Beyond high in the sky, a rainbow shone. God's smile, Father had told me before. A promise from God that good would always conquer evil, and no matter the hardship, no matter how unfair and unjust it seemed, there would always be hope.

Life spread throughout the area where darkness and death had once ruled. The once grim forest became enchanting, reborn, and I did not wish to look away.

"Incredible. How did this happen? How did you know?"

"My father, my brothers, and I came here to visit. We wanted to know what the land would look like after the mountain collapsed. You can imagine how shocked we were. I'm not sure what happened, but I think when you threw the last bean, it somehow—well, let me show you the rest."

I wasn't sure what I would see next, but I dared not blink, afraid the beauty in front of me would disappear. Never had I imagined I would witness such exquisiteness. I wondered what had happened to those treasures. Perhaps they had been buried deep within the mountain when it collapsed.

I expected to see the end of the glorious pastures and hills at any time, but they extended for miles. When Jack stopped, he helped me off the wagon. I glanced around and soaked in the miracle.

A pleasant, sweet scent filled my nose as I stood in the middle of an oversized arch of leaves and limbs. The giant trees not only bore huge leaves for a perfect shelter from the sun, but the trunks sprouted the same green leaves all the way down to the soil. Walking farther in, a honeyed sheen poked through the canopy of trees, and then more poured like Heaven's light.

Some of these trees were covered in flowers I didn't recognize. Beyond these trees were tall beanstalks, though much smaller than the one I'd climbed. To the left sat grand mountains, and my ears perked up to the tinkling sound of a waterfall cascading into a stream and snaking around the trail flanked by brambles and berry bushes.

"It's beautiful," I said. "You truly believe the bean did this?" I looked to my left and right when I did not get an answer. "Jack?"

"Turn around, Jacky."

When I did, my eyes grew wider. Jack held out a beautiful uncut sapphire, my favorite color of gem. Jack cleared his throat and took a step toward me. The sunlight kissed the tips of his hair and lightened his eyes to greenish blue. After licking his lips, he began to speak.

"I've dreamt about you being my mate since the first time I set my eyes upon your beautiful smile. I must have seemed like a pest to you, but I did not know how to act in front of girls. You made me feel like I could fly in younger days, and you still do. We've been through so much together in a short amount of time. We've even stared down death together. I don't want to waste any more time, because as you already know, time is precious. I want forever with you. I'm in love with you.

"You don't have to love me back. Just give me a chance, and I promise I'll do everything to make you fall in love with me. Your mother has already given her permission for me to propose marriage to you." Jack cleared his throat, his voice a little shaky. And for the first time, perhaps he was a bit nervous. "Will you give me the honor and allow me to be your husband? Will you be my mine forever?"

Tears streamed down my cheeks as I held my hands together to keep me steady. His words were beautiful. I had no idea he was capable of saying such things to me. Jack kept surprising me, not just with his charm, but with the good things he'd done.

There were no words to describe my feelings. My heart thumped faster, expanding from bliss, so full to the point I thought it would explode. Jack filled me with his love and devotion, and I could not have asked for anything more. I would give him that day, the next, and forever.

"Yes, Jack. I would be honored to be your wife."

Jack cupped my cheeks and seized my lips. He shouted and twirled me around.

"So, let me see that sapphire." I took it out of his hand when he released me. It was as big as my palm. "Where did you get this?"

Jack rested his hand over mine. "While we battled Longinus, my father and his men took some of the treasure out when they could not find Richard. They took it to the rock edge and threw it off. Some was destroyed in the fire along with the mountain, and some was safe. My father and his friends took the treasures and spread them to the towns the monsters had destroyed."

I nodded in understanding, recalling the little girl's words. My question had been answered.

"We thought it would be best to help the people back on their feet quickly. However, I admit I picked this one out especially for you. I was planning to make an extravagant necklace. I know you're practical, and you're going to tell me you don't need it, but I think we should think about what we're going to pass down to our children." Jack furrowed his brow, questioning.

I crushed my body to his. "You're brilliant, Jack. And I do love you."

He pulled away to meet my eyes, as if he could not believe me. "Say it again. I want to hear those three words."

I tilted my head to the sky and belted. "I love you, Jack."

To my wondering eyes, the trees began to stir. Then the flowers on the trunks burst, spinning around us like wild wind. They were not flowers as I'd thought, but instead slumbering butterflies awakening to celebrate my proclamation.

Oh, what a splendid sight.

The fluttering butterflies pirouetted in the air, their wings like a whir of silk ribbons floating about. Then they ascended to the endless canvas of blue.

"Oh, my." I watched them soar. From below they looked like tiny, colorful angels.

"I just made that happen for you."

Jack broke my stare.

I laughed. "You can believe you did."

"You don't believe me?" He chuckled. "For that I won't show you what's under the cover."

"I don't need you to show me." I pulled back from him. "I'm going to find out."

I ran around the horse, but Jack blocked me. Then I went the other way, but Jack ran faster.

Darn this dress.

"Jack, get out of my way."

"Not until you tell me you believe me."

I circled the wagon countless times until Jack caught me. Out of breath, I said, "Okay, you win. You made the butterflies appear."

Jack smirked and lifted the cover to reveal a few lanterns, another basket filled with food, blankets, and even a couple of swords.

"Your mother has given me permission for us to spend the night on the wagon. I gave her my word I would not compromise your virtue. I will keep my promise. She knew I was bringing you here. I told her how much the land has changed. I wanted you to see. I know your heart is heavy that you could not bring your father's body back to be buried. But look around you. This is where he was buried. No one has ever had such a beautiful resting place before. So forgive yourself. The last bean was for your father. You did well."

Oh, my heart. Bless you, Jack.

Tears flowed and fell faster with Jack's words, and my heart swelled from somber to heaven blessed. This was my father's grave—beautiful and breathtaking.

"You're right." I wiped my tears and smiled. "My father was buried here. I want to be married here. Let's take away the evil and make it good."

"I agree." Jack planted a soft kiss on my forehead.

Jack and I spent our time climbing the beanstalk for fun. I took great pleasure in embarrassing him as I stripped off my dress, only to reveal a tunic and breeches underneath. Though the wind nipped my nose, the need to climb gave me all the warmth I needed to ascend higher. When I reached the top, the grandeur of the town and what the last bean had created revealed its beauty.

Spectacular.

When the light faded, I lay on the blanket inside the wagon with Jack. Blankets layered on top of us to keep warm. Jack held me in his arms, stealing a few kisses at times, but he kept his hands to himself.

I talked about our wedding while gazing at the infinity of diamond specks against the black-void of night sky, so mystical, filling me with serenity and wonder. So many, and so close I felt like I could reach out and touch them, reminding me I was small and not alone in the grandness of the universe.

Then, when I could no longer stay awake, I fell asleep in Jack's arms while the angels' eyes watched over us.

Chapter Twenty-Eight
Eight Years Later

efore Jack and I married, Jack built a house for us next to my parents' home, so my mother wouldn't be alone. He also hired good men to tend to the animals and the farm for Mother. Mother only needed to oversee their work. The men would also go to town with her as her companions. No woman should travel alone.

Jack had apprenticed to a master carpenter and with his skill built a respectable name for himself as J and J Tradesmen. The first *J* stood for Jaclyn. He said he would always put me first, and he had kept his word.

His brothers also worked with him. They would playfully argue the initials stood for James and Jonathas, and we had a good laugh.

To remind the town what we all had endured, Jack designed the front of his shop with vines growing like beanstalks. Jack thought people needed to remember how precious life was and how easily it could be taken. The reminder would help people heal together, a common bond to make the town stronger.

He even had a local jeweler design a beautiful gold beanstalk necklace for me. The beanstalk curved into a circular pendant, leaving an empty space in the middle.

Upon seeing Jack's shop and my necklace, the townspeople

bought cloaks, tunics, fabrics, and hats embroidered with vines—even the fancy hats had vines made of felt instead of feathers. The bakers too rode on the trend and made bread and pastries shaped like beans and vines. The children sang songs about the giants and the beanstalk. Even after many years passed, it was still the most famous story in the towns.

As for Father's hat, I'd left it in my room at my parents' house, so Mother could look at it whenever she felt the need. It seemed silly a hat could mean so much, but we needed it to heal, bringing us close to Father, as if he remained among the living.

I might be biased, but I believed our wedding was one that would be the talk of the towns for generations to come. We had our wedding where Black Mountain used to stand, just as we'd discussed. We had waited until spring, when the weather was perfect.

It was magical and enchanting, a fairytale wedding, especially when the butterflies fluttered all around us at the end of our ceremony. I liked to think of it as a blessing from Father.

Our plan to have a small family wedding did not happen. The townspeople heard, and just like my father's funeral, came by with lots of gifts. I was sure it was their way of thanking us.

A year after our wedding, we had our first child. We named him after my father, just as Jack had promised.

"Can you tell us a story?" Richard asked, taking his last bite of a chicken leg.

I did not know how it was possible, but Richard had similar features to my father. At almost seven years old, he already acted like a young man.

"Of course." I kissed his cheek. "I have the perfect story in mind." Ruffling his hair, I turned to my daughter, who sat next to him. "Elizabeth, would you like more chicken soup?"

"No, thank you. My tummy is full," she replied in her cute little five-year-old voice, tossing her braided hair from side to side.

"How about Father?" I asked Jack. "Would you like more soup?"

"No, thank you." Jack turned to little Jaclyn sitting next to him, picking up a little chunk of carrot from her dress.

Little Jaclyn was definitely her father's girl. For a three-year-old, she was quite independent, but not when it came to her father. Jack would tease me and tell me our daughter was just like me. I had to admit, he was right—right down to her stubbornness and courage.

Little Jaclyn also had the same birthmarks and healed like me. That worried me. What the future held for her, I did not know. But I could not stop fate.

Everyone has a story to tell, Mother had said before. *Fate will lead you to a path on which you are meant to be.* And fate would do the same for our little Jaclyn, and perhaps generations to come. And she too must be brave. *I may be a woman, but women have their own bravery,* Mother had once said. And I believed it to be true. Those words would be instilled in my sons and daughters, and on through the ages.

"Would you like more soup?" Jack asked little Jaclyn.

"Would you, Father?" Jaclyn smiled, looking at him admiringly.

Jack pounded lightly on the wooden dining table he had built for eight. "Yes. We eat like giants," he grumbled with a deep, gruff voice.

The children laughed, even our one-year-old son, Jeremiah, who had no idea what his father had said. Jeremiah sat securely on Jack's lap, and Jack kept all the bowls away from him.

"Jeremiah looks just like you," I said to Jack.

The way Jeremiah's beautiful green eyes sparkled, the sound of his laughter, even the way he looked mischievous, I already knew he was going to break girls' hearts.

After dinner, while I brewed hot tea, and children sat around the fire, a knock on the door startled us. Jack got up to open the door and the children's happy voices cheered.

"Grandmother."

They all hugged her at once. Jack had to hold Mother steady so she would not fall from being cuddled from all sides.

"One at a time." Jack chuckled.

"Mother." I gave her a hug and a kiss, and then she handed me boxes.

Sometimes Mother went to town to visit friends. I was happy she did. She needed to live her life too.

Mother had bought baked pie for our family. She had just come home from visiting William and Clarisse in town. Clarisse was William's new wife and my mother's longtime friend.

"These look delicious." I cut them into small pieces for everyone. The children patiently waited at the table with their drooling mouths.

"You must visit Clarisse's bakery, Jaclyn." Mother's blue eyes twinkled as she placed the plates on the table. "She has so many different kinds. I brought the children's favorite." She looked at each of them adoringly.

"Can you tell us a story while we're eating our pie, Mother?" Richard begged with his beaming brown eyes, so like my father's.

"Aye, Richard."

It used to hurt when I called his name, and I had wondered if we'd made a mistake, but I was glad we had honored my father by naming our first son after him.

"Father will join me." I sat next to Jack and began a tale that I'd heard spreading the town. "Once upon a time, there lived a boy named Jack."

The children laughed.

"That is Father's name." Elizabeth pointed at her father with a mouthful of apple pie.

"Yes, it is." Jack gave a silly grin. "Jack's family was so poor, his mother sent him out to trade their cow for something better." He looked at me to continue.

His affectionate eyes locked on mine, and I melted on the spot.

"Jack met an old man along the way. He told Jack he would give him some magic beans that would become a beanstalk and grow to the sky."

The children's heads tilted to the ceiling when they saw me look up.

"Then what?" Richard took a bite of his pie, but kept his eyes glued on me.

Jack jumped in, "Who would not want magic beans, right?"

"There's no such thing." Richard laughed, almost choking before he swallowed.

Jack cocked a brow, and we exchanged glances with a smile. The children had no idea.

I held out my hand as if I held the magic beans. "Jack's mother was not pleased at all. She threw the beans out the window and sent Jack to bed without supper."

"That's mean." Little Jaclyn pouted, placing her fists on her hips.

She was always the one to speak her mind. Jaclyn was so much like me.

"Aye." Richard crossed his arms in agreement, as if he'd been the one sent to his chamber.

"The next day…" Jack lowered his voice for dramatic effect. "When Jack woke up, the giant beanstalk had grown to the sky just as the old man had proclaimed. He climbed and climbed until he reached the clouds. Before him was a giant castle. When he went inside the castle, treasures of plenty filled his eyes, and then…"

The children's eyes grew with anticipation.

"And then … he saw the giants."

The children's mouths parted in shock, and then I jumped in to tell the rest. I made up bits about a golden harp, a golden egg, giants following Jack down, and how he chopped down the beanstalk.

At last, their father shared the giant's treasures to help the poor and the hungry, and, of course, his own family. The children, Mother, and Jack clapped when I ended the story.

"'Twas a great story." Richard pretended to chop the beanstalk with an imaginary sword. "I'm faster than a giant."

Richard, being the typical boy, would likely fight giants later with the wooden sword that had once belonged to me, out in the field. And his two sisters would join him, especially Jaclyn. Jeremiah, being only one, would watch and laugh.

"Your mother told us many stories in her younger years. She has told you many, has she not?" Mother asked.

"She has. I love them all." Richard smiled at me adoringly. "Can we hear that story again tomorrow, please?"

"Only if you behave." Jack set the cup down after taking a sip of his tea.

"I shall." Richard licked the plate of his finished pie, and then wiped his lips with the back of his hand. "May I have another, please?"

Mother got up from the table. "I shall return."

"What's this story called?" Elizabeth held out her empty plate to ask for more, flicking away a tiny piece that had fallen on her lavender dress.

I looked at Jack and winked. "*Jack and the Beanstalk.*"

Epilogue
The End

That night, as I cuddled in bed with Jack, I dreamt of Father. It wasn't the first time and I knew it wouldn't be the last. It was said dreaming about your departed loved ones meant they were visiting you spiritually. I did not know the truth of it, but I wanted to believe it so.

I could not remember Father's words, but I awoke feeling he was proud of me. Sometimes I would awake sobbing, like I was saying goodbye again, and other times I woke with pooling tears.

Jack was always there to comfort me, holding me until I was back to myself again. The nights I dreamt about Father, I would visit his burial site behind my parents' house and talk to him. It was a way to help me heal.

I missed him so much it hurt. Sometimes I did not know if I could make it through the day, and sometimes I held my father's hat and cried next to Daniel. But knowing he was in my heart and all around me made it bearable. It was so true what people said. He might not be there physically, but he was there with me in other ways.

I felt my father's love through my children's laughter. His love had never left me and never would. His memory would live on, not just in our hearts and souls, but also through the many lives he had touched. People praised him still with talks of his courage and good

252

heart when I visited the towns. He was well loved by many.

Eight years before, when the news about my father, the monsters, and the men who'd died on Black Mountain was still fresh in people's minds, the story spread throughout the towns as a tale for children, called *Jaclyn and the Beanstalk*. However, the story had changed over the years when my children shared my version of Jack and the beanstalk.

Jack and I laughed at such nonsense, and so did the people who knew the truth.

Jack and I decided not to tell our children about what happened on Black Mountain until they were old enough to understand. In a way, we did not have a choice, since little Jaclyn was just like me in many ways. When the time was right, all would be revealed.

As parents, we tried to shield our children from the evil. We wanted them to hear and see all that was good, so they too could follow such examples.

Evil could never conquer good. As long as there was love, evil would be overcome. So my father taught me before he died, and so I would teach my children. Love was the truest savior. I believed it in my heart to be true.

The true story might never be told again. But one day, it would resurface again when Jack and I decided to tell our children. Who knew? After all, stories changed all the time, and the way towns gossiped, I'd bet this one would. They might even rename it once again...

Jaclyn and the Beanstalk.

Acknowledgements

To my agent, Italia Gandolfo, who told me I had to write Jaclyn's story and for giving me that push I needed to make it the best it could be. To, Liana Gardner, for always being there for me through every process of getting this book done. Jessica Nelson, Holly Atkinson, Jane Soohoo, Cheree Castellanos, and Katie Harder-Schauer, for your guidance and expertise for fine tuning this novel.

To Mary's angels, thank you for believing in me and for all your support.

To my bestie, Alexandrea Weis, for always being there for me and giving me great advice.

To my readers, thank you for your continuous support. Your friendship and love for my stories means the world to me.

Redd Riding Hood

Chapter One
Who's Afraid of the Big Bad Wolf

Redd

The unforgiving breeze stung my bones.

I shivered as its icy fingers clawed my nape. Even the squirrels felt the warning. They scrambled up to the intertwining branches, scampering from the last bit of sun as dusk drew near.

I wished I had listened to my instincts and begged Father to hunt another day, but I didn't want him to think I was lazy. How was I to explain the foreign sensation in my gut, cutting off my air, or that my dream the previous night had terrified me so much I awoke in damp nightclothes?

He would think I had gone mad.

Scents of pine and soil filled my nose. The familiar bumps and curves of the landscape enticed me to enter, as if to say, "Safe. You are safe to enter. No harm will come to you, boy. You have come to me since you were a child, and I have never hurt you."

Yellow and orange leaves fluttered like butterflies, swirling and dancing with the breeze. The branches were almost bare, getting ready for winter.

The snap of the twigs and thud of my feet meeting the dirt brought me back to my purpose.

My skin crawled.

Something tugged at my center again, but this time it wasn't friendly. "Leave the forest," it seemed to say. "Go now before it's too late."

The forest I loved, where I'd gone hunting countless times, became something to fear.

Why the sudden change?

I didn't know why this sensation gnawed at me, stretching and growing the longer I stayed. But I ignored it. Pushed it aside. I feared Father would think I was a coward.

Whoosh.

Crack.

I flinched and whirled with my musket raised, my back to my dad's. Something had rustled inside the bushes yards away. The leaves crunched to the left, with more shuffling in front of the bushes.

"Stay next to me." My father gripped my shirt and yanked me closer.

My heart pounded, ready for the kill. I had shot a deer before, and every time my stomach clenched, but not this time. I wouldn't let it.

I bottled up my anxiousness and told myself killing an animal was out of necessity. Winter was near and we had to get ready. I pushed aside the guilt.

Father slung the first musket's strap tightly around his shoulder. Then he aimed the second toward the bushes ahead. Father always brought two when we went hunting.

He spun to follow the deer's impossibly fast leaps. Unless there was more than one, it couldn't have covered the ground that swiftly.

I crouched low, mimicking my father when I spotted a patch of brown, and then antlers. The deer would not only provide us meat, but a new coat for my sister.

Such an easy kill.

There was no challenge. The deer held still. One shot straight to its throat would mean a quick death.

Father waved his hand toward the deer, signaling that he was allowing me the killing blow.

I've got this.

I pressed my finger on the cool metal, and then the air shifted.

Cold. Dangerous. Haunting.

Phantom claws raked over me. I shoved that feeling down and squashed it. I would not let this fear leach away my nerve or spoil my aim.

Hesitation was never good. The image of Father's frown flashed in my mind.

Not now. Not now. Not now. Do it. Shoot.

My finger tightened, ready to squeeze, but …

Father jolted up and took a step back, almost knocking me over in the process. He glanced from tree to tree.

Still on bended knee, I curled my finger around the trigger again, but the deer had gone. Father had spooked it.

I cursed, but Father's action worried me. Never had he scared away game.

Father pushed my musket down and hauled me up. "Shhh …"

"Father—"

I had used the same quiet tone, but Father covered my mouth with a trembling hand.

He pressed his mouth to my ear. "Son. When I let go, you run. Run as fast as you can to home and do not look back. Do you hear me?"

Yes, I hear you. No, I will not run. I'm eighteen. I'm a man.

I wanted to ask questions, but when his grip on my shirt tightened, I acquiesced. No time to argue when it seemed so important to him. Then his hold on me loosened, but he didn't fully let go.

A low growl from a dense thicket to my right raised the hair on my arms. My breath caught in my throat. Father must have known a predatory beast lurked about. I had been so focused on not missing my target, I had shut out all the noises around me— like looking through a tunnel at my prey.

The same guttural noise came from the opposite side, behind me … and then … A figure with eyes as red as fire, black and gray fur, and dagger-like teeth stood several yards away.

Not a deer.

Not a fox.

A wolf?

Twice the size of a wolf.

Dear God. What in heaven was the monstrous figure in front of me?

I had never seen such an enormous creature in my life. And just like that, I had turned into a scared little boy. Muscles trembling. Mouth shut. Brain useless. Heart galloping. One second earlier, I had been the predator. In a breath, I became the prey.

Go away. Just go away.

"Son. Don't move."

Father's shaky voice was hardly audible as his fingers ever so slowly uncurled from my shirt, lifted his musket, and then fired. The deadly sound echoed throughout the forest, followed by the smack of the bullet in animal flesh.

The beast howled in pain and spun to reveal blood seeping from its side. I relaxed my shoulders and released the breath I held.

Safe. The forest did not forsake me.

Then a snarl loud as a thunderous storm erupted from the wounded creature.

My knees buckled and my breath stuck somewhere inside my throat. The same sound came from my left, and the right. Rustling and thumps convinced me we were not safe after all.

I'd thought the beast was alone, but it seemed it had brought its family with him. Wolves traveled in packs. I had forgotten until the continuous guttural noise surrounded us. There had to be dozens of them.

Run. Run. Run. No. Don't be a coward. You can't leave Father alone.

Father whirled and blasted his second musket, but I couldn't move.

Help him. What's wrong with you?

I finally raised mine to shoot, but something shoved me aside.

Dirt painted my face. My palms slammed against rough pebbles and twigs. I spat out the soil and hopped back to my feet, searching for my weapon.

Just as I spun, a smaller wolf gripped father's musket in its heavy jaw and held it immobile. Then the wolf my father had wounded tore into his shoulder with his teeth and swiped a claw across his neck.

I wanted to believe this was a nightmare I would wake up from, but Father's head tumbled from his body, blood marking a trail of its direction.

The ground split open and sucked me under. I screamed, but no sound escaped.

Oh, God. Oh, God. Oh, God.

Father ...

Horror rendered me speechless. My limbs buckled. I became immobile as the boulder behind me.

With my father's blood dripping from its mouth, the wolf locked eyes with me, advancing triumphantly. Its gait steadfast, its eyes promising the same fate.

This monster didn't seem like a mindless animal, but instead a beast with purpose and understanding—more than it should.

Five wolves stood behind the larger wolf.

Shoot it. Kill it.

I was desperate to grab something ... anything to defend myself. When I eyed my musket next to the tree, another wolf pawed it to the side.

Its mocking expression seemed to say, "You're dead. You're our dinner now."

Father had died to save me. He had pushed me when the first wolf attacked. And this is how I would repay him? No. I would not die here. I would not die today.

I picked up a stick as the wolves began to pace, taunting me. The leader with black and gray fur snapped its jaws and roared. It pawed at the ground, like the way the dogs did after taking a shit. But this was no friendly gesture. Either he was performing some kind of wolf ritual before the kill, or he was giving me a warning.

I pointed my stick at him, and then whirled to the other wolves that paced near me.

Nowhere to run.

Nowhere to hide.

I was good as dead, but I would fight 'til my last breath with every ounce of strength I had left.

The faces of my mother, my little sister, and my truest friends Noah, Beth, and Ruby flashed in my mind. They would be left to starve in their own grief with Father and me dead.

After the wolves killed me, they would most likely eat me to the bone. Food was scarce in the forest; they must be starving to so boldly attack musket-armed humans.

The dark gray wolf to my left sprang, opened its mouth, and yanked my stick away. A soldier to ensure no harm would come to the leader. Once I had no weapon to defend myself, the leader wolf dove for me.

Someone help me, please.

The pack leader lunged for me.

I should have felt pain beyond measure, felt my flesh rip and blood flow. In fact, I should be on the ground and mauled by the pack.

But another wolf, with startling white fur, had attacked the leader. Though smaller, it roared like a lion and fought like an experienced warrior. Its strength seemed incredible.

They tumbled, churning up dirt and pebbles. The other wolves backed away, watching.

Do something, idiot.

I picked up my musket and pointed at the two wolves. I could have shot at the pair, maybe scare off the others and get rid of the nightmares, but I couldn't. The white wolf had saved me—I thought. Maybe it had waited for the right opportunity to attack the alpha. Regardless, it saved my life.

Coward. Shoot them all. Hurry.

I aimed my musket at the nearest wolf, but none attacked. They snarled, sharp teeth showing and jaws snapping. My instincts beckoned me to shoot, but my heart wouldn't let me. I would only kill to defend myself. Even though they had killed Father.

I fired toward the sky, hoping it would startle them. The surrounding wolves backed away, but the fighting two didn't stop. Taking my chance, I reloaded with trembling hands and pulled the trigger.

The leader wolf broke away with a jerk and a hideous yelp. It licked at a smudge of blood on its shoulder and whimpered as its soldiers circled it protectively. As a unit, they disappeared into the deepest dark shadows. The white wolf was not among them.

I hurried to search for the last wolf, fearing it would attack me next.

Red stained the beautiful white coated wolf, but it wasn't its own blood. The wolf stood on a boulder, staring at me with stunning golden eyes. Strange. Not a threat. Perhaps to thank me.

But I didn't understand why it had attacked the other wolf. Maybe they had a history. Maybe this wolf was sick of the other wolf leading the pack. Whatever its reason for being there, I thanked it.

I waited, breath heaving, my chest rising and falling as fast as the wolf's. When it loped away, I dashed toward my father.

Oh God. The horror. The blood. My father. He didn't deserve this wretched death. I would never forget the beast that killed my father. I would never forget … never forgive … my lack of courage.

My fault.

Father had died because of me. Because I wasn't fast enough. He had protected me, but I had failed to protect him.

But why had the white wolf saved me? Fate had kept me alive. Why?

I dropped to my knees, my heart shattering to a thousand pieces, dead as the leaves on the ground. Uncontrollable tears fell. The pain unbearable from my loss, the guilt tearing me apart inside and out.

"I'm so sorry, Father. I should have been braver. I am ashamed of myself."

I was at a loss of what to do. How could I explain what had happened to my family?

Kneeling in the dirt, I grieved as darkness fell upon the world. I let time slip away.

I wished I could too.

About the Author

Mary is an international bestselling, award-winning author. She writes soulful, spellbinding stories that excite the imagination and captivate readers around the world. Her books span a wide range of genres, and her storytelling talents have earned a devoted legion of fans, as well as garnered critical praise.

Becoming an author happened by chance. It was a way to grieve the death of her beloved grandmother, and inspired by a dream she had in high school. After realizing she wanted to become a full-time author, Mary retired from teaching after twenty years. She also had the privileged of touring with the Magic Johnson Foundation to promote literacy and her children's chapter book: No Bullies Allowed.

Mary resides in Southern California with her husband, two children, and two little dogs, Mochi and Mocha. She enjoys oil painting and making jewelry. Being a huge Twilight fan, Mary was inspired to make book-themed jewelry and occasionally gives it away as prizes to her fans.

www.JaclynandtheBeanstalk.com
www.TangledTalesofTing.com